In All Thy Ways

Michael Evans

ISBN: 978-1-0980-7792-1 (paperback)
ISBN: 978-1-0980-8135-5 (hardcover)
ISBN: 978-1-0980-7793-8 (digital)

Christian Faith Publishing, Inc.
832 Park Avenue
Meadville, PA 16335
www.christianfaithpublishing.com

Printed in the United States of America

CONTENTS

CHAPTER 1

Abominations Child

"Vivette, you will be there for tonight's séance, won't you, dear?"

Vivette was pruning one of her bushes in what was becoming an extensive garden in her backyard. It was one of her two obsessions.

"Of course, Myra. Bertrand and I would not miss it for the world, would we, Bertrand?" Vivette turned to her husband and smiled excitedly.

"No, not for the world," droned Bertrand with all the animation of a porcelain doll.

Bertrand's lack of enthusiasm was lost on the two ladies. Their world only made sense to them, but Bertrand wasn't concerned about what made sense any more than his wife was concerned about Bertrand's lack of interest. He did not care for such things but he would dutifully let his Vivette get her thrills from Myra the charlatan.

By all appearances, Bertrand and Vivette led a happy, successful life. Bertrand had a respectable job. Vivette had her nice house and ever-growing garden, and their first child was on its way.

"You are feeling well enough, Vivette?" asked Myra. Myra, who felt it was her celestial right, rested her hand on Vivette's belly.

"Yes, we are looking forward to our little Leo coming into the world."

Myra's eyes lit up and questions tumbled out. "After the constellation? Have you checked the horoscope? I've always felt Leo to have a fierce psychic connection? Will he arrive in time?"

"Yes, I believe so," cooed Vivette joyfully. Myra's eyes widened as she smiled broadly, sucking in air as she did so, which caused a slight hissing sound. Bertrand stifled a yawn.

Leo was born on August 22, just in time, which was fortunate for Myra, who had considered the possible ramifications of naming her son Virgo. Bertrand was indifferent to children, even one of his own, but he did his best to entertain enthusiasm because he had learned over the years the importance of keeping up appearances. He lived a lurid, secret life of which even those who knew him best were clueless and it helped that Myra was distracted by gardens, dreams, and stars.

Leo the lion grew apparently normal in spite of abnormal parenting. He seemed to have his mother's simple-mindedness but he was his father's son and a time was coming when the peaceful days of naivety would give way to an awakening of cruelty. His mother continued to dabble in all things supernatural, other than the only one that really mattered, until it got to the point that their house became overcome with charts, trinkets, artifacts, and books about the bizarre. She was dead but thought she was alive. Bertrand lived a secret life encompassing all that his wicked mind could conceive and did it in such a fashion as to be completely undetectable to all those who thought of him as quiet and unassuming. He was dead but thought it did not matter.

For the first nine years, Leo lived and played and was oblivious to the foolish and hidden depravity that wandered around him like an angel of light. He inherited his mother's deep blue eyes and his father's pear-shaped physique and pudgy face. Still, in spite of everything, Leo seemed unremarkable and as content as any boy of his age in a peaceful suburban life. He was still a blank page. Then when he was ten years old while walking home from school, everything changed. He spotted a couple of boys, two grades above him, arguing with one of the girls in his class. He stopped and watched as if he were observing a sporting event. The girl, whose name was Alma, seemed red in the face, possibly from something said to her from one of the boys. It was apparent that she was fighting back tears but instead, perhaps to prevent the boys from the pleasure of seeing her cry, started screaming at them.

"You're mean and ugly," Alma spit out.

Just then, one of the boys pushed her so hard she fell over backward, books flying and legs shooting out from under her as she flew awkwardly onto the ground. Alma gasped, partly because the wind had been knocked out of her, but mostly because of shock and fear.

"And you're ugly and stupid," sneered the other boy, whose name was Winston.

Alma scrambled to her fleet, scooping up her belongings the best she could, and fled.

The two boys laughed wickedly and that was when they noticed Leo watching. They walked up to him with the swagger of a panther as if they had just taken down a ferocious enemy instead of an outnumbered, embarrassed, frightened girl.

"Are you going to tell on us?" asked the other boy with a threatening voice. The very question implied that it would be better if Leo did not tell on them.

Leo tilted his head slightly and stared at the two boys as if the scene before him was a puzzle and he was trying to put the pieces together to see what the picture should look like. The boys at first were a little taken aback at Leo's countenance. He did not seem afraid. He seemed distracted. Winston stepped up close to Leo's face and glared at Leo.

"'Cause if you do, you'll get more than she got. You might just get knocked down and not get back up again. So I am asking you again, and if you don't answer, I will take that as a yes and you will regret it."

At that moment, the first page of who Leo was to become had begun to be written. Something strange happened. He realized that he enjoyed watching the two boys hurt the girl from his class. He could not explain why, he just knew it to be true down in the depths of who he was. Even stranger to him was the observation and realization that his pleasure taken in her humiliation should bother him because he knew it to be morally unacceptable. Instead, the fact that he knew it to be wrong and did not care brought him even greater pleasure. To hurt someone weaker, to know it was objectionable and repulsive to others, and to still take a cavalier attitude, no—it was more than cavalier he thought to himself, he took an aggressive exhilaration in her pain. Up to that time, he did not know what evil was until he had seen it in himself.

From that day forward, Leo found himself collecting methods of causing emotional pain toward others weaker than he. Always weaker. It was not because he was small and fearful of bigger, older, and meaner people. He was big himself and not afraid of anyone who wanted to challenge him, but the pleasure he derived from hurting someone equal or greater did not bring him the same sadistic thrill that came when he pulled the wings off the harmless, powerless girls who came across his path. He was a contented monster.

Of course he was bound to be noticed. An inexperienced boy his age was certain to be caught. Soon he was known in school by the others students. Later it was found out by the teachers, and after that, it quickly came to the parents' attention. At first, Vivette, easily persuaded by her sons denials and pleading, staunchly defended her dear Leo because the idea was simply beyond her grasp. Bertrand remained silent, knowing that the source of his son's behavior was no different than Vivette's outwardly expressive foolishness or his own hidden carnal gluttony. However, as the truth of Leo's ways became more obvious and less deniable, Vivette dove deeper into her plants and idols while Bertrand withdrew deeper into oblivion.

Leo, unlike many deviants, did not gain added satisfaction from being found out. Getting discovered deprived him of pursuing what he loved most and so he learned over time to become a master of eluding, lying, and misdirection. In short, he became his father with the exception that he chose cruelty over perversion.

The family continued in its secrets, but Vivette was troubled. It wasn't just Leo's behavior at school that bothered her. He frightened her. There was something about his countenance, which almost made her afraid to be in a room alone with him. It seemed silly to think that she felt unsafe with her own child, which was why she did not confide her fears with Bertrand. However, she felt it impossible to keep anything from Myra, who visited often, whispering vague spiritual incantations and encouraging Vivette to grow in the dark arts by drawing deeper on unseen forces. The only thing that Vivette seemed able to grow was her garden which was slowly becoming more of a jungle. Myra pressed her with the idea that it could somehow become a modern Garden of Eden that might bring the spiritual answers Vivette needed. They would spend many hours in the garden considering the possibilities.

Bertrand and Leo continued unabated by a correction they saw no need of receiving and felt no desire in obtaining were it offered. It was toward the end of Leo's teen years that an unusual change took place, which would spin the three into separate worlds. Bertrand developed scabs on his hands.

At first it appeared as a minor rash and he sought medical aid which provided some creams to attempt to restore his skin to its normal condition. It had no effect and within a few months both hands had been completely covered. Doctors were baffled. Bertrand was in no pain but it was difficult to use his hands and it became too unsightly for him at work. He took a temporary leave of absence and spent his time alone in his room. Vivette found the sight hideously macabre, so much so that she moved herself into the spare bedroom. Leo was busy tormenting innocents, so the last thing he was interested in was his father's hands. For Bertrand, evil seemed to be on hold while he waited out this strange malady.

Then one night, Bertrand noticed that the scabs were peeling. They had previously been very thick and hard as concrete. Up until then, the temptation to pick and peel at them was as fruitless as trying to peel the skin off of a rock. But now they felt soft and itchy. Bertrand poked and then awkwardly with two scabbed fingers tried to pull on a flap of one of the scabs. A small piece broke off. Bertrand, encourage, continued to pick, poke, and tear at his left hand in the dark, the scab remnants falling on his bedsheets. About half way through something seemed strange to Bertrand. He stopped clawing at the scabs and brought his left hand closer to his face. He had finished pulling the scab off the back of his hand and had just

9

pulled away a large piece on the palm of his hand. He assumed he would see either a white or raw pink hue to his skin but he could not quite figure out what color his hand was. It seemed to change as he moved his hand. He reached over and turned on the lamp with his right hand and pulled his left hand close to his face and looked at the palm. He could not figure out why each time he turned his hand the appearance of his palm changed. He needed a better view.

Bertrand walked to the bedroom door and flipped the light switch which controlled an overhead light. He lifted his left hand up with the back of the hand toward the light. The skin seemed white now whereas it had appeared to be much darker when he was sitting on the bed. As he rotated and moved his hand about he suddenly stopped and gasped. A wave of nauseous horror enveloped him as he realized that the whiteness of his skin was in fact the view of the ceiling light pouring through his hand.

For the first time in his life, Bertrand experienced something other than bold passivity. He always believed in wrong and right. He chose that which was wrong. It appealed to him. He also believed it had power whereas that which was right was weak. No matter how much righteousness might desire to exact retribution, it lacked the power. For this reason, Bertrand always treated it with a cavalier bravado. Now he realized that he had grossly underestimated its horrifying nature. He lifted his trembling right finger, still covered in scab and attempted to poke the palm of his left hand. There was nothing there. Strained guttural sounds came uncontrollably out of his mouth as he continued to push his finger forward. There was no resistance as his finger continued through his palm and out the back of his hand. He felt sick and decided to sit down on the floor.

After what could have been minutes or hours, Bertrand stood, turned the light switch off and stumbled in a daze slowly back to his bed. He stared at the bedsheet and the scattered scab remains. For a moment, a wave of rage rushed through his body and he felt the temptation to fling the bedsheet and smash and throw anything he could get his hands on. Instead, he let the rage pass, reached calmly toward the night stand light switch and pulled the chain. He slowly pulled the bedsheet back and eased into bed, letting the darkness envelope him.

Bertrand had told himself that if one day he was judged that it wouldn't matter. Nothing mattered. That was his philosophy. Perverted, secretive pleasure was all he was interested in and he knew a day would come when his body, like all others, would cease to function and he would be done. He did not believe in life after death, but he realized it was possible for him to be wrong, but no matter, the grave held no threat to him. It occurred to him that he was ready for Hell but he was not ready for this horrid destruction. He was not prepared to face his insignificance.

He stopped picking at the scabs. Leaving ugly, uncomfortable scabs seemed a far better alternative to losing his hands. Unfortunately, the itching became unbearable and he lay in bed trying to think of anything other than tearing away at his hands. He spent the night tortuously fighting the temptation to scratch and claw. Eventually toward morning, he passed out from the exhaustive task of self-denial. When he awoke, he yawned and after a few seconds of ignorant bliss he remembered his situation and looked down at his hands. They were gone.

He stared, stunned at the ghastly sight of his two forearms ending handless at the wrist. His bed was covered in scabs. At first he assumed that he must have scratched his hands uncontrollably in his sleep but he noticed two small pieces of scab remaining on his right hand. As he looked at them closely they fell softly to the bed. He then realized that it would not have mattered if he had scratched his hands or not. The scabs would have eventually fallen off anyway. The conclusion was fruitless when it came to giving him any peace of mind.

"Bertrand, will you be having breakfast?" called Vivette from the other room.

Bertrand was startled. The activities of the night had caused him to forget there was a world outside his door with other people leading what now seemed normal, enviable lives. The night had made Bertrand famished but how to eat was a problem. It was not just that his hands were invisible. They were gone. Regardless of this new state of humiliation he lacked the humility to confide in Vivette.

He may be petrified but he was not broken. However, it was difficult to hide the terror he felt as he spoke.

"Could you please bring a plate in for me, dear?" he called out. He tried to sound warm and carefree but there was a definite strain in his voice.

Vivette enjoyed hearing Bertrand call her dear. Any intimacy in their relationship had ended years ago and it reminded her of when they were first dating and he would call her all sorts of silly romantic names. She also heard some anxiety in his voice which was almost as foreign to her as his warmth.

"Is everything all right, darling?" It was hard to resist calling him that. She realized that she missed the old Bertrand.

"Yes, it's just that my hands are a little irritated this morning."

Vivette blanched at the thought of seeing Bertrand's hands. There was something unnatural and fearful about it. She did not want to go into his room and see them but at the same time she wanted to help, so she determined that she would do her best to not look. Opening the door, she walked toward Bertrand, determined to fix her gaze only on his face. She did such a good job of concentration that she never noticed that his hands were under the covers nor did she see that the bedsheet was covered in scabs. She smiled at Bertrand while setting the tray down on a table next to the bed. She then turned and walked quickly away.

"I have some watering in the garden to do if you do not need me for anything else."

Bertrand started to answer but Vivette made a hasty retreat. It was a relief to Bertrand that she didn't press the issue of his hands. He slid his wrists under the sides of the tray and carefully placed it on his lap. He stared helplessly at it, realizing for the first time just how important his hands were in his daily routine. There was only one thing to do. Bertrand leaned over and ate his food like a dog.

While Bertrand secluded himself in the bedroom, Vivette attempted to go about her daily rituals as routinely as possible, but in truth, and this was a word that had often eluded Vivette, she was… troubled. As she watered the plants in her garden, she wondered what exactly was happening to Bertrand with his scab covered hands and also with Leo, who seemed to spend less and less time from home. The disturbing complaints from school had stopped but there was a way about him that frightened her just as much as Bertrand's scabs. She had often turned to her horoscopes and Myra for answers and support but lately they left her with a sense of something; something disappointing that she could not quite put her finger on. The beliefs she had clung to had brought a deep sense of infinite possibilities and realities. Now it appeared that so much of what she relied on was in fact finite and vacuous. The mysteries of the universe seemed stymied when it came to enlightening her about Bertrand's hands or her son's unexplainable behavior.

The garden had grown considerably in a relatively short period of time. It almost felt like a small, exotic jungle. She had attempted to import rare plants from around the world as part of her garden obsession, but many died once out of their native environment. Some, like the Cobra Lily surprisingly managed to keep going.

Suddenly Vivette leapt into the air. Something had rubbed past her leg just skimming her ankle. She looked down and saw nothing, but she felt certain that something had touched her. She quickly turned off the water and went inside the house. She stood at the window, looking into the garden to see if there was anything moving around. Even though it did not feel like fur, she attempted to calm herself with the thought that perhaps it was the neighbor's pesky cat which had wandered in. In any event she was in no hurry to explore and decided when Leo was home she would ask him to look around.

Bertrand had never been one to concern himself with what had happened, what was happening, and what would happen, but now it seemed to consume his thoughts. What was this strange condition that had robbed him of his hands, what could he do about it, and would it spread? Each question had its degree of uncertainty culminating with the last question being the most serious and consequential. It had now been a few days since he had lost both hands and he remained in his bedroom. Vivette continued to bring breakfast, only now she left it at the door and walked away after opening it. She was clearly upset by his behavior and wanted to avoid all conversation and observation. It was just as well. Bertrand had no answers. Only a growing sense of dread. After a week scabs appeared on his feet.

Time can crawl or fly by depending upon one's needs. For Bertrand, the sand was speeding down the hour glass. What was left of him was piling up on the bed in a grotesque mosaic. He had not eaten in two days. Vivette had left food but Bertrand had found it too difficult to maneuver his way to the door. She would call out and ask if Bertrand was okay and he would answer, but Vivette lacked the courage to face Bertrand and Bertrand lacked the fearlessness to face Vivette. With just a head and torso remaining he finally yelled out in desperation to Vivette.

"Yes, Bertrand," she answered from an adjoining room.

"I need you," said Bertrand with an anxious strain in his voice that Vivette had never heard. Vivette walked to the door, leaning her head near the slender opening.

"Bertrand, what is wrong?"

"I need you to come in and see me."

"Do I have to?" said Vivette, her voice cracking somewhat.

"Please."

Vivette slowly opened the door and turned her head toward Bertrand just enough to have a glimpse of him sitting naked on the bed. She froze when she saw Bertrand's gaunt face. What she saw horrified her. His hair was gone and black circles surrounded his eyes. One ear was missing. Unable to turn away, she felt as if her head were in a vice, forcing her to gaze upon the man she used to know. Her eyes moved down toward his hairless chest covered in patches of scabs. That was when she noticed that his arms were missing also. A noise came out of her, which was a mixture of dismay, disgust, and shock. At first she did not recognize what it was or that it had come from her. By then she was looking at the bed where Bertrand's legs should have been. Instead, scab fragments covered the sheets. In spite of the macabre appearance, all that Vivette could think of was that they reminded her of lilies on a pond. Her hand clutched the door handle.

Vivette took one last look at Bertrand's disfigured and tormented face before she flung open the door and ran out. She ran straight into the garden, gasping and turning in circles, straining to comprehend what she had just seen. Just then something brushed past her leg and she looked down and saw the head of a black snake. As she stared at it, the snake twisted its head toward her and paused. Vivette stood paralyzed in fear and disbelief. It seemed impossible but somehow the snakes head resembled that of Myra's. A few days earlier, Vivette had been told by Leo that Myra had stopped by and was waiting for her in the garden, but by the time Vivette had gone to the garden, Myra had apparently left. The snakes tongue flickered and it moved on. Its width was enormous. It continued slowly past her leg and seemed to keep going. Vivette knew she should run but her body would not respond. She could feel the snake now on both sides of her almost as if there were two snakes. In horror she realized it was the same snake just slowly coiling its massive body around her. She felt as if she was in a nightmare unable to make herself wake up. All she could think of was one word—"lies."

She felt a firm hand grab her and pull her quickly into the house. Her foot caught the step leading into the house and she fell forward. She could hear the door slam behind her. Vivette stood up quickly, expecting to see Leo, for she could think of no one else who could have helped her. Whatever she had been through with Leo was lost in the desire to cling to him and sob. She stood, reaching out to the hand that pulled her in but when she looked up no one was there. Except for some groans coming from Bertrand's room the house was empty and silent. For some reason this last unseen measure was more terrifying than either Bertrand or the snake. At that moment Vivette abandoned all reason and hope and bolted toward the front door with only one remaining coherent thought. Flee! Flee from this spot, flee from this house, flee from anything, everything, even her life if possible.

At first, she ran down the center of the street, oblivious of whether there was any traffic, which fortunately there was not. She felt as if she were screaming but no sounds came out of her mouth. There were no neighbors outside, which would have made no difference to Vivette, for she saw nothing and no one. Objects appeared as undefined shapes. She recognized enough not to run into anything.

At the end of the street she continued between two houses, past their yards, and into an open field. Her arms were flaying wildly and she was gasping for breath but she could not and did not want to stop. As the sun was setting she was still running through tall grass and weeds. Eventually she collapsed in a field of clover, breathing heavily, her body covered in sweat, dirt, and blood from numerous falls. Her shoes had fallen off long before and her feet were bloody and raw but she did not notice. She lay there, unable to move, her chest heaving and her face pressed heavily on the dirt, wanting the ground to swallow her up. Swallow her whole, fill her mind with the earth and let the worms eat away her tormenting memories. She longed to die and remember nothing, forgetting and forgotten. Exhausted and broken, she fell into a deep sleep.

Vivette awoke in the early morning surround by clover. For a moment she had forgotten all about her troubles and fears and felt light and carefree. She could hear singing nearby and it sounded so inviting she just lay there calmly trying to make out the words. Then her body started to shake. It had been a cold night and had she had not been so exhausted from her ordeal she most likely would not have slept so soundly. The memories of the previous day flooded back along with the incredible pain and exhaustion that pulsated through her body. She had no strength for fear or flight. Her chest was pounding and she felt as if she had a fever. The singing continued.

She lay there for some time shivering, listening to the singing and trying to make out the words. She recognized them as hymns being sung in a church but since she had only been in a church once in her life the melodies were foreign to her. She tried to lift herself up but collapsed back onto the ground in pain. She used one hand to brush away some of the clover and arched her neck as high as she could and saw a cross on top of a small church nearby. As she did so the voices seemed to be a little clearer and the sounds and the cross brought back the one memory she had of ever being around such a lovely sound.

Vivette was ten years old when her mother had taken her to visit her aunt for the first and what turned out to be the last time. Until now Vivette had completely forgotten about the experience and the resulting anger her mother bore toward her sister. It had been a beautiful day and while Vivette's mother slept, the aunt asked Vivette if she would like to visit her church where they were having choir practice. Vivette did not know what a choir was but she liked the woman and anything seemed more interesting than sitting around the house waiting for her mother to wake up. So the aunt left a note and the two headed down the street toward the church.

Vivette did not understand what they were singing about but she enjoyed the melodies and was fascinated with the joy of the choir. Everything about the event seemed to speak of an unknown beauty that these people possessed. After about thirty minutes of uninterrupted practice the back door of the church flew open and Vivette turned to see her mother's silhouette in the doorway. The choir stopped while her mother stormed toward Vivette. Vivette had never seen her mother so angry and was afraid that she was going to be punished. Instead, her mother grabbed Vivette's hand, whispered through clenched teeth some words to her sister and firmly took Vivette with her. They left town as quickly as they could and Vivette's mother told Vivette to never mention her aunt or the incident again. Vivette never understood why her mother was so angry.

As Vivette lay in the field, snippets of hymns drifted out of the church.

> *Just a closer walk with thee, Grant it Jesus is my plea"*
> *Just as I am without one plea but that thy blood was shed for me*
> *When peace, like a river attendeth my way, when sorrows like sea billows roll.*

Just as when she was a child, Vivette was keenly aware that she did not know what the words meant but the same sensation of beauty covered her like a warm blanket and she gradually stopped shaking from her chills. It was strange to her that words which had no meaning to her brought more peace than anything she had ever sought or experienced. How could such a thing be? The moment this question came to her mind she felt as if she were really asking it of someone and almost immediately she sensed she had an answer. She remembered when Leo was an infant. Like all infants he cried sometimes and she would murmur some soothing words to him and after a few minutes he would calm down, his beautiful blue eyes looking up at her with complete fascination and trust. Even without understanding the words he was comforted. The illustration brought a smile to her face because she knew somehow it had come from the one whom the choir was singing of.

Did I just pray? Vivette wondered. *Was it really that simple?* It had always appeared so formal and uncomfortable when she saw others praying. Bertrand used to mock those who prayed. *Poor Bertrand*, Vivette thought. Down inside, she knew that such a horrible fate must be the result of something he had done. Without wanting to confront him, she always suspected that he had kept secrets from her and now she shuddered to think what they must be to have caused such a disturbing judgement. Praying and now thinking of judgment. What was happening to her? All her life she had searched the unknown and now the unknown one was making himself known to her. And it was all lovely and filled with beauty. Not just draped or immersed in beauty, it was beauty. It was something she realized that she should have sought and not some mystical deepness found in the stars. The stars she had studied never revealed beauty to her, only an endless search with never ending questions, unanswerable and unsatisfying. If she had sought for beauty she might have returned to this. Tears rolled down Vivette's face. She had been a fool. All she wanted now was what she was hearing. Could it possibly be hers in spite of her foolishness? The words were so glorious. The originator of beauty had to be forgiving. Otherwise, how could he be beautiful? She closed her eyes and listened.

Her body was found two days later, her death the result of a heart attack. Bertrand's body was never found and no one could explain the mess in his room. Leo took over the house and asked no questions. Frankly, he just did not care. He cleaned out the room and ripped away the garden. Myra was never found but a large snake was discovered dead in the garden, its head crushed by a large potted plant. It was another mystery that no one sought an answer for.

Leo finished school, living in the house alone, living off the insurance money from his mother and father. Eventually, he needed to work and found an opening at a women's correctional facility in a neighboring town. For a while, he assisted in the offices running errands, but in time, he became a guard. He spent his years tormenting the prisoners. He was called the Toad by those he abused, though not to his face. In the end, he was known and remembered by none, save his victims.

CHAPTER 2

The Watchman

Time flies, time stood still. Sometimes time seems to be everything but what it is, constant. For the old man, there was a time when the days were short and filled with activity and the nights even shorter because they were accompanied by a deep and restful sleep, but the old man's time had changed as much as his locale. Now his day was as long as the highway in front of his house and his sleep as barren as the desert he lived in, but the contradiction had become a blessing in disguise.

Insomnia has its benefits for those who watch and pray. Since the old man seldom slept, when the early morning desert sun broke through the thin veneer of shades into the room, he was already up and standing in front of the oversized window which faced the older unused highway about thirty feet away as well as the newer highway a few hundred yards behind. The window was another one of the contradictions which existed in the old man's life. Most noticeably, it was relatively new compared to the rest of the building which, like the old man, had survived many years and many visitors. The window was meticulously clean and free from even the smallest of scratches whereas the walls supporting it were old, worn, and had a faint perpetual odor of oil and gasoline. It was the type of window that might be seen in front of a small department store, or as in this case, a retired gas station. It was the only serious renovation that the old man had made to the gas station, which he had purchased about a decade earlier. Seeing clearly had become a priority for the old man who was waiting and watching, for it was the Watchman he had become.

As he pulled up the shade, light from a demanding sun flooded into the room with a rush as if to declare its ownership of all the nooks and corners of the darkness. The desert heat quickly pursued like a mobilized army following its leader into battle. As the heat permeated the room the stench of gasoline and oil seemed to saturate the air and seep into his pores causing the hairs on his arms to briefly stand up and then, after the tidal wave of desert fury had run over him, settle back down. The Watchman had spent most of his life in places that were cool, comfortable, and many miles away. But the desert howl had beckoned him and while he was not impervious to the irritations that accompanied a solitary, nearly unlivable and desolate existence, his life and vocation had taught him how to endure and how to wait, especially when there was a purpose.

He had bought the old gas station for next to nothing. The previous owner, a man named Gus, had gotten the cancer and decided to move north to spend his last days with his brother. He had been on the verge of abandoning the station anyway, which had become an increasing burden to him. He had spent most of his hopeful teen years and pitifully dull adult life behind the once shiny gas pumps or in the back garage under some car or another needing some type of repair. When he was younger he would commute back and forth to his apartment in town, but as time wore on, he would simply sleep at the station until finally, by default, it had become his home. As a young man he had almost married. She was his childhood sweetheart, but the young lady with the long auburn hair and smile that made his knees buckle, abruptly changed her mind, claiming she wanted to go to the city first and get a college degree. He patiently waited and wrote long love soaked letters scattered with poorly worded poems. Months went by with nothing in the mail but letters marked "Return to Sender" and he concluded that she had gotten cold feet, or maybe she just realized all she would get out of the marriage was a lifetime of free auto care. After a year, it was painfully clear to him that she was never coming back. He threw away the photo on the nightstand, thoroughly burned the now embarrassing letters, and gradually lost all interest in a life spent with anyone other than random customers.

There was another reason that Gus was eager to sell. Since the new super-highway had been built, fewer and fewer motorist used the old highway. At some point he suspected the old highway would most likely be closed. Gus had not prayed much in his life, but he felt that the old man's proposition to purchase the station was an answer to a prayer he had never actually got around to asking. He was a little surprised when the old man told him that he intended to convert it into a house but Gus simply nodded his head in agreement. If this stranger wanted to purchase a rundown gas station in the middle of nowhere and turn it into a house, who was he to discourage such a notion. This piece of junk property had wasted so much of his life and rewarded so little, so if the well-manicured elderly gentleman who looked like he had never lived a day in the desert wanted his gas station for a house then he would gratefully take what he could get and quietly recede away from the heat, isolation, and meaningless memories.

After a simple bill of sale and a friendly handshake between two men who each thought they got the better of the deal, Gus slid into his truck and peeled away in a trail of dust never looking back. The Watchman turned and stared at what was now his.

The main room was the front room that faced the highways. Originally it had been the front office where travel weary customers paid their bills and bought necessities and odd assortments to help them pass the time on the sleepy highway. With the new owner, the room changed from a cluttered mess of sundries to a sparse four walls and floor with little to show for it other than the bare necessities a man might need to get through a day of watching and waiting. The floor was partially covered with thick scattered throw rugs of various sizes so depending on the temperature he could use them at his discretion. The coolness of the cement floor reminded him of his childhood when on a hot summer day he would walk to the lake near his uncle's house and stand ankle deep in the water. A single bed lay against the wall opposite the large window. On cooler seasons, the Watchman would leave the shades open and lie in bed on his side staring outside the window; watching, waiting, and wondering if he she was still alive and what it would be like if he saw her again. Then he would fall asleep and dream strange dreams about what had happened and what might happen.

There was no closet, just a large mahogany chest of drawers up against the wall opposite the foot of the bed in which his few clothes and various blankets were kept. At the head of his bed was a small inexpensive bookcase which contained some medical reference books, a few of his favorite classics such as Swift's *Gulliver's Travels* and Ellison's *The Invisible Man*, and a few Bible reference books. Sitting on top of the bookcase was a reading lamp, telephone, and a notepad and pen. A small red refrigerator squatted against the wall opposite the chest of drawers with a six foot wide Formica table separating the refrigerator from an electric stove to which he had added some shelves below it to hold his few cooking tools. The last piece of furniture was a simple oak table on the left side of the window and a single chair facing the outside view. On the table was a bowl of walnuts and an open bible with the Watchman's reading glasses and a pen resting on the top page. Next to the bible rested a 35mm viewfinder camera ready to go with six shots left on the roll. A door opposite the foot of his bed led to the bathroom. Kitty corner to the left, a door opened to a darkroom, which the Watchman had set up to develop any unusual photographs he had taken.

On the grimy, grit-stained back wall of the room above the bed, taped firmly with masking tape, hung an odd collection of black and white photographs. At first glance they appeared to the casual observer to be a very uninteresting and repetitive set of photographs of landscape as seen from the front window. But they were as unique as the Watchman. The pictures were taken at different times of the day under various climate settings. The best ones, for reasons known only to the Watchman, were taken with an overcast background or in the early evening. The landscape itself was of little interest. It was bland at best, with very little of the plant and animal kingdom in view. Occasionally, a wandering tumbleweed would pass by, sometimes pausing as if to pose for a picture and then playfully move on. Mostly it was barren land with no rise or fall in the terrain. Vehicles would pass by and every now and then someone would pull up to the front of the house thinking the gas station might still be open even though the pumps had been removed. Perhaps it was because of the large rectangular stone that sat stubbornly just off the old highway about fifteen feet in front of where the pumps had been. It had become somewhat of an iconic landmark to those who had travelled the highway. It was convenient for sitting and taking rest stop photographs. Like the Watchman, who sat with his Bible and camera, it was waiting for something more purposeful to unfold.

To the casual observer, the old man was as unremarkable as the desert. It was the photographs that transformed the ordinary into the fantastic. What made these otherwise dreary pictures unusual and part of the contradiction of the Watchman's unassuming identity was that upon closer inspection, it was apparent that there was a faint yet defined string of dull whiteness near the center of each photograph which looked similar to the chalk outlines drawn of victims by the police. The difference was that these outlines were standing up as opposed to lying on the ground. They appeared to be alive and within the thin pencil glow of the white outline, slight features could be barely detected. Haunting shadows of eyes could be recognized with a magnifying glass. On some, the shape of the head looked as if it was turned sideways and the white lined profile of the face was highlighted. Some of the ghostly outlines of the hands were open while others appeared to be clenched perhaps in a paralyzing fear or intense anger.

A few of the pictures revealed the figures with knees bent either defensively against some onslaught or in a state of flight. Not all of the photographs were of single characters. One of the photographs had a couple standing still side by side holding hands. One faint one was of a small child. The most revealing photographs were those that had been taken with a darker background. One mysterious photograph stood out from the rest. The center of the picture was an uneven white oval shape. It was surrounded by the scene of the desert which he had come to know so well over the years. On the left side was the large iconic rock. The outline of a figure appeared to be kneeling on the left side of the rock facing toward the large oval shape. Upon closer inspection with a magnifying glass the Watchman could make out faint outlines within the oval shape. He could see a cluster of figures, some familiar in the sense that they had the shape of people, but some looked differently than anything he could identify. It was more intriguing than frightful and the Watchman liked this picture more than all the rest because it produced more questions than answers.

In front of the house he had set up a small motion sensor. The sensor was a little ahead of its time so he kept it camouflaged from the infrequent nosy visitor. Early on he had discovered that the sensor would go off when it appeared there was no movement outside. He learned that just prior to the phenomena a slight imperceptible movement would set off the motion sensor. Whenever the sensor was triggered, a green light which the he had set up inside the room would briefly flash, giving him just enough time to grab his camera and take a picture.

The Watchman stared blankly for hours, as frozen as the desert landscape, unaware or uncaring about the time. While he sat, he would casually crack open a walnut and shove the shell's pieces to one corner of the table. He had taken a large water bottle from his refrigerator and would periodically draw on it. Occasionally he would read his Bible and sometimes make a note in the margins. At one point while he sat reading, the green light flashed and he instinctively reached for the camera. An old pickup truck lumbered by and the Watchman released his grip on the camera and went back to reading.

The hours passed with the Watchman alternating between sitting, staring, reading, and every so often he would stand and stretch. The Watchman did not feel bored or restless. He had waited for years and he was determined to wait for years to come if need be. He believed that there would be a conclusion. He had not been called for naught. One thing however that could not wait was his need to eventually use the bathroom. The Watchman stood, wiped his desk clean of shells, and walked to the bathroom. Just as he stepped inside and closed the door, the green sensor light flashed.

CHAPTER 3

In Transit

The bus driver had been driving the commercial bus for almost fifteen years. In those years of driving, he had seen all types of passengers from all walks of life. The rich, the poor, those riding with a purpose, and those who had found their purpose in running away. Some were kind and generous, some not so much. Once, a well-dressed man with a brilliant red Cadillac whose transmission had blown gave him a thousand dollar tip for stopping and offering him a free ride to the next town. Most, however, were simple, common folk riding the bus because it was the cheapest way to travel and were often the nicest people he had ever met. Each one might easily have a legitimate reason to complain but instead they offered smiles and thanks.

Some passengers put on airs. Embarrassed by having to stoop so low as to ride the bus, they would lift their head up slightly when he greeted them and walk silently down the aisle as far as possible, hoping that if they went far enough they might find themselves in a more acceptable vehicle. At times, while driving, he could feel the disdain of passengers, like a magnifying glass burning a hole in the back of his neck. It often puzzled him that anyone could be so infatuated with the idea of disliking him for how he made a living. He had learned over time how to handle the rude comments, the monotonous complaints, and the overused clever insults. He had learned the art of being immune to meanness.

With a few exceptions, he was content. He never had false hopes or even high aspirations. He thought of himself as a simple man with a simple life. Even in his younger years before the joy of driving a bus was a reality, his expectations for what he might achieve or become were casually bypassed. It was not as if he had never thought of the idea of "making something'" of himself. He had considered the notion of a higher education or trying to find his way into a lucrative field. For about fifteen minutes of his life he had even considered joining the army but he disliked exercising and the idea of physically confronting someone with the intent to kill repulsed him. It was not that he was a pacifist or that he lacked patriotism. He just knew he did not have it in himself to do the hard deed. As a worker he was not lazy and he was not adverse to some sort of promotion or a degree of recognition. He knew that if he wanted he could do more. He simply didn't want to. As far as a vocation was concerned, he was joyfully complacent.

The company he worked for, Transit Plus, at one time had been a serious competitor with some of the bigger bus companies in the southwest area, but had in the last five to ten years been steadily declining in business. A lackluster style of management had failed to keep up with the times. Older buses were being forced to run with a gambler's mentality as to their trustworthiness. Many of the buses still did not have air-conditioning or if they did it often blasted air that was hotter than the desert heat. The founder and president of the company had owned a number of lucrative businesses in the automotive related field. It was his specialty and his passion. Those traits combined with a rigorous work ethic made him extremely rich. He had five children still living when he suddenly died of a massive stroke and each had received the key to the car, so to speak, of one of his businesses. Of the five children who inherited the businesses, four of them were similar in character to their father. Their businesses continued to not only thrive but expand, aided with the introduction of new blood and new ideas made for the times.

Transit Plus fell into the hands of the youngest son. The son was much like the storied prodigal son in the Gospels who takes his inheritance and decides to squander it on riotous and selfish living.

The difference was that Transit Plus had not quite reached the point where the son was ready to come to his senses and while the company bled green the son was joyfully content to roll around in the mud with pigs. The underlings for the son, the ones who had known, loved, and respected the father could see the writing on the wall. Some tried to right the ship while others jumped. The sycophants crossed their fingers. The one feature that kept Transit Plus still operating with any semblance of strength was that they were the only line willing to still take routes that others felt were too out of the way to earn a sufficient profit.

The bus driver, not knowing all these details but living off the office gossip, was justifiably nervous about this and wondered and worried more and more about what he would do if the company let him go. He was contented to be a bus driver, but it was another story to be an unemployed one and the option of working for another company was geographically problematic. Not to mention his age and skill set which kept his options limited if he was forced to try something different. These ponderings and others even more troubling occupied his mind while he drove the quiet desert highway.

One thing the bus driver had learned from seeing countless passengers tromping on and off his bus was that many had at one point experienced some type of tragedy or sorrow and if they had not, he had been around long enough to know that someday they would. Sometimes a young child would board the bus with a bright grin and carefree manner and the bus driver would wonder how long it would be before their heart would be broken or their world would be shattered. It seemed unfair yet inevitable that every child was born for misery. *How well would they handle it?* he wondered, as they smiled their way past him, racing toward a window seat on the bus. How well had he handled it?

The bus driver was an only child who had grown up happily in an almost nonexistent small town, which never exceeded four hundred souls. His father ran the only store in town selling everything from groceries to hammers and nails. He had purchased the store from a Frenchman named Jacque many years ago who had the brilliant idea of naming the store after himself, so "Jacque's" it was for decades. Somewhere in those decades the sign which bore his name was blown off its hinges during a terrific twister and disappeared into the night. Neither Jacque nor the bus driver's father saw the need to ever replace it.

If you wanted anything you went to the store with no name and no sign or you travelled fifty miles to the next town, which was larger and had a sign. The town was more akin to a large family than to a small community. There was one doctor, one teacher, one church, and no sheriff. There had never been anything more serious than petty crime which when it had happened was never much of a mystery to figure out the who, the why, the what, and the when. Most of the younger ones left when they were done with school but enough stayed so that it always seemed that the population remained relatively the same. For some, it was paradise. For others it was a prison with an open door and bus pass when their sentence was up. Families understood when someone wanted to leave and did all that they could to help. They understood that not everyone was the type of person who could live what seemed like a very small life. At twenty years of age, the bus driver was working at his father's store wondering what type of person he was.

In the end, he decided he was a little of both. Transit Plus bus lines would make their stop in the small town occasionally. It was not a regular stop because of the size of the town, but whenever anyone was visiting or someone had purchased tickets or called ahead Transit Plus would be there. The young man mulling over his future had gotten to know the talkative bus driver whenever he had pulled into town and stopped at the store. One day the driver mentioned that he had to make a return trip to town that night and wondered if the young man would like to drive with him and keep him company. The young man had never been on the bus and thought it would be fun to get out a bit.

By the time he returned that night, it seemed as if the clouds had parted and a light had shined down upon him. Being in the bus felt right and comfortable, like a new pair of shoes that fit just right. The driver rambled on about a girl he had started to date but as the young man walked down the empty aisle resting his hand briefly on the seats the driver's voice trailed away, and the young man imagined a bus filled with passengers while he sat confidently in the seat taking them to their destination. It was where he belonged. It spoke to all of the simplicities that appealed to him. It lacked complications and gave him a sense of purpose. It felt simple and important at the same time. It also allowed him just enough of a leash to stretch his legs but not stray too far. Some people in town wanted to get as far away from their roots as possible. The young man who was to become the bus driver wanted to get just a little away for just a little while. He also liked to sit.

The young man's father hoped that his son would continue the work of the store but like most parents in town he had already made his peace with the possibility that it might not happen. So when his son poured out his heart about what he wanted to do, the father gave his unconditional blessing, and with that, the young man trained to become a bus driver and was eventually hired. At first he took any odd route offered but after a few years a convenient route opened and he settled into a consistent schedule which allowed him to check in regularly with his mother and father.

His schedule enabled him to be home on Sundays. He would get in late Saturday night from a run and sleep at his parent's home and then go with them to church the next day. Late one Saturday night he had pulled his car in front of the house and noticed that the doctor's car was also parked nearby. The drapes to the living room were opened and he could see his mother sitting on the couch with her side facing him. She had her head buried in her hands and the doctor was sitting next to her with one hand on her heaving shoulder. A cold dread came over the young man. He was not ready for death. He wanted to drive away without being seen, hoping that when he came back everything would somehow be reset and he could pull up and see his mother and father in the living room with his father sitting comfortably in his favorite chair reading the paper. Instead, he sat frozen staring at his mother until he realized that his mother was staring back at him. He could see her tear stained face in a painful contortion of sorrow and grief. He forced himself to open the car door and hesitantly drag himself toward the house, his legs feeling like lead weights. It was only his mother's face which kept him from fleeing. It was the first time he had ever felt his heart pierced so deeply and his body gripped with such paralyzing fear. His father was dead. He opened the door to the house where he and his mother wept through the night.

For the next few months, the young bus driver pleaded with his mother to let him quit his bus route and take over the store but she adamantly refused. She argued that his father would not want him to leave what he loved out of a sense of duty or guilt. "All would be fine." She would sell the store to a recently married young couple. She had her friends and her son had a good job. He would continue to live with her and help out as needed. She said she was at peace and nothing would change her mind. So the young driver, with a somewhat decreased sense of guilt but increased sense of responsibility resumed his routine. His current route was usually at night. His seniority with the company gave him the option of riding the day shift, but he preferred the night shift so that he could be home during the day with his mother.

Life settled back to a somewhat lonelier sense of normal. His mother was active with her friends and church, but he could see that her joy was fading. Her energy seemed to have waned and her attention often drifted away to some distant time and place. It was a slight alteration which only her son was able to detect.

His behavior also changed, albeit somewhat different in nature and something only his mother noticed. He often seemed distracted and depressed. One day after church as they were walking toward the exit to greet the pastor at the door, the son stopped. A man in a brown suit was standing on the other side of the pastor staring blankly at the son. The son stopped and his face turned white. His mother turned toward him and asked him what was wrong.

"I need to use the bathroom," he answered. "I'll meet you at the car." The mother proceeded toward the door and greeted the pastor. When she reached the car she noticed he was already in the car waiting.

"What was all that about?" she asked.

"Nothing. I felt nauseous for a moment but it passed. I decided to leave through the side exit."

The routine of life continued, as it does whether hampered or unhindered, and one Saturday night the bus driver was finishing his shift for the week. The next morning he would faithfully go to church with his mother and then nap for the afternoon after one of his mother's early Sunday suppers before going back to work at night. Normally on a Sunday night the load was pretty light but that night the bus was almost full. As he drove toward his last stop he looked into the mirror and noticed most of the passengers had their eyes closed either sleeping or at least giving it their best attempt. He enjoyed the quiet of the desert at night. He knew that would be a strange thing for someone to try and understand, because even during the day the desert could seem quiet, but the bus driver had lived his whole life in the desert and had a subtle appreciation for the changes in the seemingly unchangeable wasteland. Sometimes he felt the desert was more alive than the passengers on the bus. As he drove he kept the headlights on high beam. Traffic was minimal on a Sunday, plus more and more drivers were starting to use the newer highway.

The bus driver was staring lazily ahead at the narrow beam of light coming from his bus when he saw the man in the brown suit standing in the middle of the road.

Passengers cried with a start as the bus veered sharply to the right, skirting off the shoulder of the road and onto the desert floor. A pop was heard and it was clear to the driver that a tire had been blown. He clutched the wheel tightly, trying to keep the bus under control as it skidded and also to keep his hands from shaking. He pulled up about fifty yards and found a place to park in front of a gas station.

"What's wrong with you?" yelled a man from the back. "What happened?"

The bus driver looked down at his hands which felt as if they were melded onto the wheel. Sweat beads had started to form on his forehead. Soon it felt that his body was covered in sweat. Volumes of perspiration ran down his neck and back. His mouth experienced the opposite effect. He tried to swallow; only he couldn't get his throat to work. The voice from the back repeated itself.

"I said, what's wrong with you?"

He tried to steady his voice as he spoke.

"Sorry, everyone. There was a dog in the road."

CHAPTER 4

Elena

Elena had been sleeping fitfully when the bus swerved wildly to the right. The sudden motion of the bus caused her to nearly fall into the isle. Instinctively, she reached out with her left hand and grasped her mother's forearm, almost pulling her down with her.

Her mother firmly pulled her back toward her without uttering a sound. She had not been sleeping when the bus swerved, but staring blankly out of the small bus window into the empty night. With all the commotion from the startled passengers, she was one of two passengers who had not instinctively reacted to the sudden jerk of the bus. Elena looked at her with a mixture of fear, surprise, then awe and wonder. The aloofness to everything she encountered was always a marvel to Elena. She was the type of person who never seemed to be bothered or anxious no matter what the circumstance. The few who knew her, knew very little. If asked, they would probably say she was even tempered. Her calm demeanor belied the fact that she simply did not care anymore.

Elena gave her mother a wondering look and the mother knew from Elena's expression what she was asking.

The mother tiredly turned her head back toward the window and said plainly, "I think there was a dog in the road. The bus driver has pulled over."

Elena quickly abandoned any safety concerns and anxiously looked out the grimy window, hoping to see something of a dog about, but other than the faint outline of a gas station and a large bench-like rock she could only see the covering of night. She worried that the dog might be hurt or worse. Some of the passenger's windows were down and she listened intently, hoping she could hear some kind of sound from the wounded animal. However, with the chaotic noise within the bus pouring forth from the angry and startled passengers there was little hope that a whimpering dog could be heard. Even if the clamor had quieted she sensed no outside sound would penetrate the bus. There was an eerie stillness in the blackness that appeared unrelated to either the tumult going on inside or the normal nighttime desert sounds outside. It reminded her of a phrase she had once heard from an old woman who lived two floors down from their last apartment. Elena and her mother were walking down the stairs to the exit when the old woman's door flung open and the old woman sprang out like a cat pouncing on a mouse. They had lived long enough above this slightly lonely and deranged woman so that neither of them was shocked when she flung open the door and like a prophet of old proclaimed with one finger pointing toward the heavens, called out ominously, "The dead of night. That's when they come. The dead of night."

Elena's mother ignored her out of habit and they continued to move down the stairs. The phrase intrigued and frightened Elena and she often pondered its possible meanings. Was there a life and death to night? She would conjure up images of dead things at night. Did night itself hold the power of death? Did the dead come at night to capture whomever they sought? She wondered if this is what that old woman meant when she uttered those words. For the first time it occurred to her that a deathly silence could be so thick and demanding of attention that no amount of noise could detract it from the authority of its presence.

The disturbing dead of the night silence had detracted her from the possibly injured, possible dead dog and she felt a need to change her thinking before she frightened herself to death, so she decided to examine the other passengers in the bus. It was a perfect time to do so. There was so much confusion and activity with busy heads and bodies turning every which way that no one would notice a small girl watching. So while they talked, complained, pontificated, and postulated, she used the opportunity to observe without notice.

She first noticed a stocky man in a suit about two rows from the back of the bus who was gesticulating wildly with his arms, talking so fast that all she could make out was "no time," "big money," and "big trouble." His jacket had been folded up and it was resting on the back of the seat like a small pillow. Even in the dark his pale skinned face was red from anger and she could see a vein in his neck which looked ready to burst. His sporty red and yellow tie was crooked and loose and the top button of his dull white shirt was open. Elena could see faded yellow stains under his arms and decided to look elsewhere.

She turned to the front of the bus and saw a young man sitting very still in the front seat, leaning against the inside wall of the bus with his legs crossed, resting on the seat. He had jet-black hair, which was neatly combed straight back. He had forceful eyes and a firm jaw with a slight smile. He almost seemed amused by the activity of the other passengers. His face had no lines, as if he had quite literally never had a worry in the world. He looked distant but entreatable at the same time. Just as Elena was musing over how out of place he seemed in the midst of the clamor around her, he slowly turned his head and looked directly at Elena and smiled. Elena quickly looked down.

She kept her head down, afraid to look up in case the stranger in the front was still looking at her. She decided to close her eyes and concentrate on what the other passengers were saying. She had heard once that when one sense is missing the other senses get stronger; however, being a mute since birth she had never noticed her hearing getting any better. She could only pick out pieces of conversations between some of the closer passengers.

"We'll have to wait all night!"

"What kind of fool risks our lives over a dog?"

"Doesn't he know that I have to be back by morning?"

Eventually she picked up some helpful information. Apparently there was a flat tire but no one could change it because the one flashlight the bus driver had was not working. The gas station had been sold and was currently an empty shell of a building, so there would be no tools or help found there. Unless someone drove by to help, they would be stuck for the night until it was light enough to change the tire. Elena decided to open one eye and slowly looked back at the stranger. By now he had closed his eyes and appeared to be resting or asleep. She decided not to press her luck. She felt that possibly he might know she was looking and open his eyes so she decided to turn her head and look back at Henri.

Elena did not know Henri but she had heard the man next to him speak his name. Henri was the only one on the bus who was close to Elena's age. Unlike the stranger, she was secretly hoping that Henri would turn and look at her but instead he was straining his neck left and then right to look out the window. She hoped he would turn around and smile at her but he only seemed interested in finding a dog.

Elena lifted the small chalkboard she kept around her neck that she used to communicate with others and placed it on her lap. She pulled out a short piece of chalk that she kept in her blouse pocket. It was too dark to see much of the chalkboard, but the marks of white chalk stood out in the darkness around her. Elena attempted to draw a picture of a dog.

She started to sketch the tail, wondering if it should be the tail of a happy dog wagging or of a frightened dog cowering in fear. While she was trying to decide her mother stood up and cut across into the isle. She barely turned her head toward Elena as she spoke.

"I'm going to smoke a cigarette. I'll be back in a few minutes."

Elena desperately wanted to go with her but fought the urge to grasp her mother's hand. She did not feel safe in the bus with the angry passengers but she knew from the expression on her mother's face that she wanted to be alone. It worried Elena sometimes that her mother always wanted to be alone. The idea that someday her mother would want to be alone so badly that she would leave forever frightened her. At the moment, though, it did not frighten her as much as a bus filled with angry adults, so she gave her mother a desolate look. Her mother seemed to barely notice Elena's pain and anxiety as she rummaged through her purse.

"I'll be right back. Just sit and draw."

Elena gloomily watched as her mother walked to the front of the bus, pulling a cigarette out of her case along with her lighter. After speaking briefly with the driver a moment, the door opened and Elena watched her mother walk down the steps. Elena hoped she would turn around and smile at her. Somehow everything would seem all right if she would just turn around and smile. Her mother paused at the bottom step and lit her cigarette, her shoulder and head still visible to Elena. Please turn, please smile, Elena silently pleaded. Please come back. Without a glance her mother disappeared into the night and was gone. Elena put her head down and tried not to cry. She looked at the slate and the small piece of chalk in her hand. She would draw the cowering dog. Her hands moved slowly and as she drew she felt that the stranger in the front seat was watching her.

CHAPTER 5

The Ghost

The ghost was not a ghost. Or maybe it was. The bus driver was never certain. He could not tell if the ghost was real or whether his guilt was so great that it had made the ghost real; in time he realized that it did not really matter. The effect of the two possibilities had merged into one collective haunting. Reason had no more power over a ghost than it did a guilty conscience. Reason could not stop the apparition from appearing at any moment, whether it was at church, in the market, on the road, or in his recurring nightmares. When the ghost appeared, the bus driver tried not to look into its face. That was often unavoidable since there was no warning of his appearance. When he did see the man, he saw kind eyes and a somewhat confused expression, staring back with a sort of Mona Lisa smile on his face. He could not tell if the smile was one of devious revenge or patient understanding, which was what made the ghost appearances so unbearable. The bus driver, like most, assumed that an angry apparition would be more frightful, but the haunting look of this gentle demeanor unnerved him more than any hideous monster could. It was here that reason was equally inept in that it failed to halter his oppressive guilt. It was unbearable and the bus driver became convinced that the ghost was pursuing him and he was certain that sooner or later it would catch him and like a chicken being chased down for supper, the ghost would grab him and snap his neck. That, he pondered, might be the end of his guilt but it also would be the beginning of his descent into madness.

Whatever the ghost-like image was, about a decade earlier it had been a living man. The living man was an average man, one of no distinction or position. What did stand out was his name, which was Auberon. His mother had read the name somewhere in a book and felt it had a strong sense of nobility. As a child, Auberon did not share his mother's fondness for the name since many of his peers thought his name had a strong sense of humor. In time, possibly because he was noble after all, he learned to live with it.

Auberon sold life insurance and spent many hours on the road. He had a good sense of humor without being a loud, guffawing, back slapping huckster with one hand shaking the client and the other hand shaking him down. He was tall with a thin but sturdy frame. He liked dark brown suits and his only vice was an early onset of baldness that he attempted to creatively cover with the last remaining wisps of hair.

Auberon genuinely loved selling life insurance for a living and hated the negative connotation that often came with salesmen. As a result he was known as a trustworthy salesman and customers often referred him to friends and family. Sometimes he responded to inquiries called in, such as the day he was sent out to a farm near a remote village. A widowed father was hoping to get some life insurance for his daughter's sake. As Auberon was pulling up the long dirt driveway toward the front of the house he could see a young woman sitting on the front stoop. The moment she saw his car start to pull in she jumped up and briskly walked toward the car. With about ten feet left between them, she sternly crossed her arms and blocked his way. Auberon turned off the ignition and stepped out of his car.

"That will do. You've made your trip and now you can get back into your car and make the trip right back where you came from. There will no selling of insurance here."

The wind was blowing and Auberon had forgotten all about insurance. He could only stare at the woman's face, somehow even more beautiful in anger. She had long red hair and the wind gave it a wild appearance matching her temper. She was waving a finger at him now and had started to make threats about how she would have him removed but all he cared about were her captivating brown eyes. He could not take his eyes off of them. Eventually, she realized that the salesman wasn't listening to her but only staring at her with a dopey grin.

"Now, Molly, you just let that man in. I called him. Not you."

Standing on the stoop was Molly's father. Molly stood for a moment meeting the salesman's penetrating stare, not sure what to make of it, but then quickly turned around and walked toward her father.

"You do not have to get life insurance for me! It is absolutely foolish. I will not have it."

"I will hear the man out, Molly. He has taken the time to come out and he seems nice enough. It would be rude to send him off. Now could you please get us both some tea?"

Molly stormed into the house slamming the door behind her. Her father chuckled as he watched the young man park his car and get out.

"Just like her mother," he chuckled again. "Just like her mother. Name's Hector," he said as he reached out his hand.

"Auberon, but you can call me Joe. That's my middle name. It's a little easier."

"All right, Joe, come on in."

One thing Auberon had learned about people was that they liked to talk even if it wasn't the most agreeable of conversations. He let Molly pour out all of her reasons to her father and him about why she did not want her father "recklessly throwing money away." He actually was in no hurry to stop her because he found he was not only entranced by the way she looked but he loved the sound of her voice. Eventually Molly ran out of steam. She had exhausted herself. That was when her father stood and faced Auberon.

"I have to work on some fencing out back. I'd like you to hear what this young man has to say. He certainly has listened to you." The father turned and smiled to himself. He could already see what these two would find out in time.

Auberon watched the father walk through the kitchen and out the back screen door. He turned his gaze back on Molly.

"Well?" said Molly.

Auberon started to talk. Instead of talking about policies and premiums he found himself pouring out his heart about how he felt about what he did.

He felt convincing strangers to do something for someone they loved by buying life insurance was the last act of expressing that love. You never bought it for yourself. It was always for someone else's benefit. It was the last gift you would give and it was proof that your life had the legacy that you had loved at least one person. It was the last impression a person might leave. People often talked about leaving a good first impression but seldom about leaving a good last impression. To refuse it when one had the means was an indication that if that person could not take their money with them, then no one would have it. Auberon always felt it was a kind of sickness to withhold money at death. To save while one was alive was prudent; to give when one had passed was healthy. To do otherwise was emblematic of a sickness he recognized but could not explain.

There was a long pause when Auberon was finished. He stared awkwardly at his fingernails. He had not expected to pour out his feelings about life insurance. It sounded so silly now as he recalled what he had just said. What was he thinking? Who has feelings about life insurance?

He quickly shot at glance upward at Molly. He wasn't sure what to expect. Possibly laughter, even worse, pity. It seemed only moments ago he stood confidently outside admiring everything about her and now he felt absolutely stupid.

Molly was doing neither. Instead she had a look on her face which appeared to be halfway between wonder and enlightenment, as if a new and surprising truth was presenting itself to her. After a moment, she stood and walked purposely to the kitchen door. Though he could not see her, Auberon could hear her call out to her father. Then Molly poked her head around the corner of the kitchen and smiled warmly at Auberon.

"Would you like some more tea?"

Within an hour of meeting each other, the father had his life insurance policy and within a year the man who loved life insurance married the woman who loved the man who loved life insurance. Their plan was to move into a small apartment and save for a house. They were hoping to buy a house before having a child but neither was too disappointed when that plan fell apart. A child was on the way. So they stayed in the apartment and still saved the best they could while they waited for the child to be born. Auberon worked longer hours and weekends in an effort get enough money to put a down payment on a house.

One day while on a sales call many miles away, his wife went into labor and was driven to the hospital by a neighbor. When Auberon found out that his wife was in labor he drove as fast as he could to get to the hospital in time. On a long stretch of desert highway he had not noticed the sharp piece of metal lying in the road. As the driver's side wheels ran over the hazard, he heard two loud pops one right after the other. The two tires quickly emptied and Auberon carefully pulled the car over. His worst fear was realized when he stepped out of the automobile and saw he had two flat tires. Knowing he had only one fully ready spare there was nothing to do but wait and try not to get angry that he would most likely miss the birth of his first born. At this late hour on this desolate road, the salesman knew it might be awhile before he saw another vehicle, but he was happily surprised when he saw a bus coming down the empty highway. He tentatively stepped a little into the road to try and flag the vehicle down.

The bus driver had been nearing the end of his first year of driving. Each day he felt more comfortable not only in driving the bus, but in dealing with different types of passengers. He had never considered himself a people person, but to his surprise he found that he not only got along with people but he had a natural adeptness with customers who were not so congenial.

It was a quiet late afternoon and the sun was just starting to set as the bus driver was reaching the end of a long slope in the road. It was the end of his shift and the bus driver was taking the empty bus back to the depot. He had the "out of service" light on and was enjoying the view. He normally did not like to turn the radio on while customers were on the bus. He discovered early on that not only did he have particular music tastes but so did everyone else and the moment the radio came on so did at least half a dozen requests and complaints. In the end it was more trouble than it was worth. But now was a good time. He reached over to turn the knob and as he did he noticed that a black leather wallet was poking out from under his seat. One of the customers must have dropped it and unknowingly kicked it out of view.

With an attempt to keep one eye on the road the bus driver reached down to retrieve it. He reached down and was just able to get his thumb and forefinger around the corner of the wallet. He briefly double checked the road as he started to pull up the wallet. As he did, the wallet hit the side of the bottom frame of his seat and then dropped back down, sliding a little further under the seat. The bus driver groaned and reached down again, leaning a little further down while he stretched his arm and fingers as far as they could reach. He felt the wallet and pinched it tightly with his thumb and fingers. When he sat back up he suddenly saw a man directly in front of the bus. Instinctively, the bus driver attempted to veer sharply to the left. His heart pounded and he cried out as he felt the tires slide and then lift a little on his side. Why in the world was the man in the middle of the road? His hands clutched the wheel as he tried to adjust back to the right to keep from tipping. It was then he realized that the man was not in the middle of the road but that he had allowed the bus to drift toward the shoulder of the road when reaching for the wallet.

The bus righted itself and the driver thought he might be in the clear. But he wasn't. He felt a dull thud on the right bumper. A shudder like a lightning bolt ran down his spine, through his legs and down to his feet. He could feel a throbbing in his chest and temple. Breathing heavily and shaking, he pulled over to the shoulder and put the bus in park.

For a few minutes, he sat there with his hands locked on the steering wheel. He could feel cold sweat beading up on his forehead and then rolling down his face. He knew he should go out and check on the man but he could not seem to make himself move. He looked at his hands, red from clutching the wheel. The wallet had somehow landed neatly on the dashboard. For some reason, this seemed to jar the bus driver out of his frozen state and he released his grip on the wheel. He reached out and grabbed the handle to open the door of the bus, unable to control the shaking of his hands. He dragged the door handle toward himself and opened the door while he simultaneously pulled himself up to a standing position. His legs wobbled and shook as he stood and he thought briefly that he might pass out. He pushed away the sweat running into his eyes and stepped heavily onto the desert floor, looking uneasily toward the back of his bus.

At first, all the bus driver could see was the man's dark brown automobile, almost black as the sun was starting to set. The car slanted to one side and he could see that two of the car's tires were blown. The bus driver walked around the automobile but could not see the man. Then he noticed some feet sticking out from a bush about fifteen feet away.

A feeling of death hung in the air. He went to the man who was sprawled on his back with his arms folded across his chest. It reminded the bus driver of his dead father lying in the open casket at his funeral surface. He was expecting some gross disfiguration with arms and legs twisted in some unnatural fashion, but when he saw the man's body calmly on the ground he thought it might not be so bad after all. However the man's head was partially covered by a bush. The bus driver could see some red through branches but the only way to know for certain was to pull the body away from the bush. He felt paralyzed once again but braced himself and grabbed the man's ankles and pulled. The body felt heavier than the bus driver was expecting. The phrase "dead weight" came to his mind and he almost got sick. He pulled the man away from the bush and saw an expressionless face staring back. His sparse hair was strung haphazardly around the man's face and head. It was matted with blood and the eyes that looked back at him appeared lifeless. The bus driver knelt down beside the man and shook him gently, repeating the word "sir" a few times, but there was no response. He clumsily tried to check the man's pulse but could feel nothing. The bus driver buried his head in his hands and wept.

As he sat there in the dirt and the sweat with tears mingling with sweat, a voice spoke to him from somewhere deep inside. It was a commanding voice which began pushing all thoughts and fears off to the side. He had seen a customer one time at the bus station, a large man as solid as a tank, push his way to the front of the line without a care for who was in his way or what they thought of him. They were tossed left and right like bowling pins. The customer had to get on a bus that was leaving and he was not going to be deterred. This voice reminded him of that man. It pushed and bullied fears and reasons away and demanded the attention of the bus driver. The voice was crystallizing a thought in the bus drivers consciousness that something must be done. The bus driver felt powerless against this voice and in some ways was relieved that some direction was being given. The voice started to reason with him. It stated the facts. The man was dead. The bus driver had killed him. Regardless that it was an accident it would ruin his life. People would not care nor understand. He would lose his job. He would go to jail. His mother would no longer have his income. She would lose her house. She would be disgraced. His life and his mother's life were ruined. The voice was dogmatic. It did not present these thoughts as possibilities to consider but as facts to be acted on. But what could the driver do? Then the voice said three words, "Hide the body."

Before the bus driver could ask how, the voice seemed to dig deep into the bus driver's memory and remind him of a place a few miles out where his friends and he sometimes hung out when they were teenagers. It was a canyon that was filled with small caves and dugouts. The bus driver even remembered a thought he had at the time that if someone ever had to hide something they could stuff it in one of the small caves, cover it with soil and rocks and it might never be found.

The bus driver stood. The voice, like the customer he remembered, had bullied itself to the front of the line and was getting what it wanted. Call the voice whatever eased the conscious, self-preservation or survival instinct, but it convinced the bus driver and he made the decision that hiding the body was what he wanted. He grabbed the man's legs and pulled him back to the car and for the next few hours he moved faster and with more purpose than he thought possible. When he had hidden the body and the car, he scoured the road for a sharp object. He found a long piece of broken pipe with a sharp end and used it to puncture one of his tires. Then he changed the punctured tire with the spare. Hopefully, if asked, this would help explain the delay and his disheveled appearance. He would explain the dent by saying that he had hit a dog.

CHAPTER 6

Elena's Mother

It seemed a lifetime ago that she was known as Catherine Arden Edgeworth. Her life was as rich and full as her name but those days had been taken away and now she was just Kay. She was a defeated woman with an unwanted child riding in a broken down bus somewhere in the desert night. As she stepped off the bus she took a long draw on her cigarette and stared into the darkness as if it were her own soul.

"A perfect end to a perfect day to a perfect life," she said into the silent night.

Her legs were stiff from sitting on the bus so she decided to walk a little down the road before getting back on the bus. The stretching of her legs and the comfort of her cigarette reminded her of smoking with friends at parties while they lounged around enjoying meaningless conversation and silly gossip. Smoking was a weakness for her, not for any health reasons, but because it seemed to be the one thing that connected her to her past and at the same time mocked her for no longer having a past. It stirred that part of her brain that recalled the enjoyable moments she tried to stifle, for even the good memories eventually led to the horrible ones. She closed her eyes, arched her neck, and tilted her head back. Like erasing a chalkboard, she wiped her mind clean and emptied her thoughts, a practice she had learned to master. She stood still for a long time—thinking nothing, wanting nothing, knowing nothing. She did not care about life and she did not care about death. She was unaware that the cigarette fell from her fingers to the ground.

She opened her eyes and put her hand to her mouth to take another drag from her cigarette. Her hand came to her mouth and she parted her lips to inhale. Her fingers touched her lips and it was then she noticed that the cigarette was gone. She looked down at the ground and saw only the pavement. That was strange, she thought to herself, as she turned around in a circle fruitlessly surveying the ground. She decided to head back to the bus but when she did she was surprised to see nothing but the long road receding into the darkness. The bus was no longer in sight. Had she walked that far she wondered? Maybe, she reasoned, because of the darkness she was unable to see it. She started to walk back in hope of eventually seeing the bus and reboarding. Then it occurred to her that it was not as dark as when she had left the bus. In fact it was not dark and it was not light. She thought to herself that it was more gray, like a fog, but not quite. Everything nearby was visible but not the type of visibility that is revealed as the result of light. It was as if light was not needed.

She tried to walk back in the direction of the bus, but she felt like the child at a party who is blindfolded, spun around and must then pin the tail on the donkey. Her bearings were completely in disarray. It felt to her that she had walked for miles before she realized that she could not possibly have strayed that far. She wasn't sure what to do. Nothing seemed the way it was supposed to be. Unsure what to do, she continued to walk. For some reason, which she could not explain, she felt delightfully free from any anxiety regarding her circumstances. A thought in the back of her mind whispered that this might be death. The thought did not frighten her. Life had cheated her. Maybe death would be kinder.

Time seemed incalculable. It might have been hours. It might have been decades. There was no sense of space or time. In spite of the constant walking she was not tired and felt as if she were in some kind of hypnotic, yet lucid trance. At some point, without a conscious effort she did something strange. She began to think about herself.

It started when she looked down at her dress and was reminded of when she was a small girl. She had been playing on her grandfather's farm, the farm she and her family visited every summer. They would drive from the city and spend a month on the farm while other family members, cousins, nephews, aunts, and uncles would come and go. At some point they would all be together at the same time and grandfather would have a big party. There was laughter, games, stories, and no one seemed to have a care in the world. She had forgotten how much she would laugh. She had one cousin who was very good at imitating family members and would entertain everyone with his impersonations. The feeling of tears coming down her cheeks from laughing so hard felt so real she touched her face.

Until then Kay had suppressed thoughts of her past but now she felt powerless to stop the flow of memories. The family gatherings reminded her of later years. Her father had done very well in the stock market and their family not only moved into a much richer part of the city but their friends and acquaintances also took on a richer tone. As she grew into her teen years and later as a young lady she became accustomed to elaborate parties with high society friends. She would attend, wearing the latest hat and gown where she and her friends would spend most of their time in silly gossipy laughter as they flirted and talked nonsense. Though void of any wonder or purpose it was idyllic fun. That was when she met her husband. At one of the parties.

"Pigs and whores," she suddenly screamed into the air.

She stopped and put her hand to her mouth. It felt as if someone had splashed cold water on her face and awakened her from a deep sleep. What was I thinking, she scolded herself. She had at one point not only refused to ever speak of him again but had refused to even think about him. She was startled by the sound of her voice and the guttural bitterness that came out. She also felt that it was the first time she had really spoken in years. Her voice sounded real and not mechanical. There was also a strange sensation that it was not just she who had spoken. Even though it was her voice and her thought it seemed that someone or something had declared it even more forcefully than she ever could. It was as if she were merely echoing a voice and an authority much bigger than herself. She stopped walking. She had never thought much about whether she believed in God or not, but if there were a God, He had just made a resounding cry of "guilty." A great peace came over Kay for the first time in her life. She took a deep breath and exhaled.

Even though she was not tired, she decided to sit down on the pavement. She stretched her legs out and leaned back, resting on the palms of her hands. Some gravel pushed into her palms but it did not bother her. She felt like a little girl sitting on a sandy beach on a breezy, sunny day with nothing to do but watch the waves roll in. There was no sense of fear about her circumstances or the haunting reflections of the pigs and whores who had been in her life. After closing off the room to these memories for so many years it was refreshing to open the door and windows and let the fresh air in. Kay felt a tremendous freedom from the pain of suppression.

Kay thought that she had been in love at the time. Maybe she was. She felt she was, but after only a few years of marriage she could sense a distance and strain in their relationship. There were no arguments. There was also little communication. Their sole communication centered around what she had done or bought with her friends and his work day. They were joylessly patient with each other. The idea that she had drifted into a loveless marriage bothered Kay, but she was too afraid to even broach the subject. What if he thought their relationship was fine. It might be, she thought, that perhaps this is what a marriage was supposed to be. So she continued to shop and he continued to work but neither continued to love.

One day she had come home with some new hats. She set the boxes on a coffee table and started to pull off her gloves. Kay stopped when she heard a voice. It was her husband. Surprised to hear his voice, Kay started to call out his name when she heard a woman laughing. She froze. No wild imaginations passed through her mind, only the obvious one. She slipped off her shoes and walked quietly to the bedroom door. The door was ajar just enough so she could view her husband and a woman through the slit on the hinge of the door.

Her heart sank when she saw her husband and his mistress sitting on the bed, the sheets up to their waist while they leaned on the headboard. She looked down at the floor, embarrassed, almost as if she had stumbled across two strangers. She started to turn away when she heard the mistress say her name. She froze. Her face felt flush. A surge of anger swept away any embarrassment. "What right did she have to mention my name?" she wildly screamed within herself. Filled with indignation and curiosity she pressed her ear to the small opening. They were laughing. Then the voice of her husband started on a long list of Kay's faults, methodically numbering them off one by one. One of the characteristics that had attracted her to him years ago was his wit and dry sense of humor. In time, she saw it more as cutting meanness. Now it had been turned on her. Every time an adjective was uttered the mistress would giggle. Dull, shallow, unimaginative, vapid, foolish. One comment after another cut Kay like a knife. Her knees started to buckle. Then her husband started making comments about her skills in the bedroom and with this his mistress went into a convulsion of laughter. Kay felt rage build up inside her. Not only was she being cheated on but the vulgarity of their mockery was more than she could bear.

She flung herself madly into the room. There was a wall shelf near the door that contained books pressed together by heavy iron bookends shaped as cupids. She seized the nearest cupid by its out-stretched foot and cast it wildly at her stunned husband, narrowly missing the mistress. The mistress screamed, quickly scooping up her bare essentials and raced out of the room. There was a brief calm, like the eye of the storm, where husband and wife, betrayer and betrayed stared at each other. Then they both heard the front door slam as the mistress left. The husband attempted to calm his wife with stuttering reassurances but she could see nothing but her own degradation and rage. Rage at being made a fool of. Rage that others were laughing and she was not in on the joke. She was the joke. She reached across the mantle and fiercely clutched the other bookend and this time cupid's arrow found its mark, not to the heart, but to his left temple.

Then it was over. His life and her adrenaline dissipated away. Kay sat down with her back to the wall under the mantle. Every drop of energy had drained away. Eventually, when she had enough strength, she cried, then wept, then sobbed and shook until her strength again drained away. Then she called the police.

Her father's wealth and connections kept Kay from the front pages of the press and allowed her to get the best lawyer money could buy. It also, in a corrupt judge's shady back room, kept her from the death penalty. Catherine Arden Edgeworth was given a ten year prison sentence. As much as possible she spent her time in prison alone. She hated those around her and she hated those she had left behind. She hated herself. The only reason she did not take her life was a strange stubbornness to survive, one which she could not explain. She refused visitors and in time they refused her. Unbeknownst to Kay, her father's health and business declined and about half way through her sentence he died, leaving behind the remaining money to his name. It would not be much, but when she was released it would help her move and find a place while she looked for work.

With about a half year left on her sentence, one of the senior guards took advantage of her. His name was Leo but everyone called him Bossman. Secretly the woman nicknamed him the Toad. He was an ugly, cruel man who preyed upon the female prisoners. He was secretly ridiculed and hated by the inmates but openly feared. His face was pudgy and pasty, and even though he was not that strong, he was large, and once his arms encircled someone, it was like being captured by a human Venus flytrap. In the midst of this human ogre were two pearls of beauty. Soft, round, blue eyes which deceptively gave the impression of kindness. One convict summed it up when she said, "He could be handsome if he weren't so ugly." In this monster of a man his eyes were strangely out of place. However, as a result, new inmates were often misled into trusting him which usually turned to his advantage.

It was a game of cat and mouse with the guard as the prisoners did all they could to try and keep their distance from him. One night Kay had been daydreaming while walking to her cell and found herself trapped near a closet just as the Toad was walking by. Caught off guard she tried to turn and run but one of the Toad's fat hands caught her arm and he pulled her to himself while he covered her mouth with his other hand. He pushed her hard against the wall, using his weight to hold her against the wall while he clumsily grabbed the handle to the closet door. Once open, he pushed her into the small room, still keeping one hand on her mouth. He closed and locked the door. Then he turned his attention on Kay and his eyes lit up with a hideous greed. He put one finger to his mouth, warning her not to make any noise. Then he removed his hand from her mouth and slowly lowered it to her throat. One squeeze was enough to let Kay know that should she resist, the hold on her throat would tighten enough to kill her. Once the humiliating experience was over, the Toad laughed and winked one of his deceptively evil eyes at the woman who was now crouched on the floor in the corner.

Six months later, Kay was released from prison and three months after a daughter was born. When asked what the mother wanted to name her, Kay turned her face toward the wall and wept bitterly over her pain for the last time. She was determined she would never again express the wretchedness she felt. The nurses waited awkwardly. When it was apparent that the mother would not answer, one of the nurses wrote the name Elena on the birth certificate, a name which meant "shining light." It was hard not to look into the face of the child and think otherwise because Elena looked just like her mother with one exception. She had the soft, round, blue eyes of the guard. The nurses thought she was one of the loveliest babies they had ever seen but every time the mother looked into her eyes all she could see were the sadistic eyes of the man who had raped her, laughing and winking at her. Mocking her, just like her husband. Just like her friends. Just like the rest of the world. She despised all of them. It was too difficult not to despise Elena also.

Catherine Arden Edgeworth, stripped of her dignity and now known simply as Kay, stood up from the highway pavement. Having lost all sense of time she had no idea how long she had spent reliving the horrors she had vowed to never think of. Somehow in this place it was possible to view memories objectively, almost as if they were not her own but a story that someone had told her. It occurred to her for the first time that the one person who never laughed at her was Elena. Quite the contrary. In spite of the fact that she had, at best, tolerated Elena all these years, her daughter seemed to almost worship her. In the clarity of this strange environment the mother saw her relationship from Elena's perspective and not her own. Elena deserved better. She had never blamed Elena for her misery but she realized that she had allowed Elena to think that it was her who had caused her mother's pain.

"Poor Elena," the woman whispered. "I'm so sorry."

Just then she looked up and saw the bus.

CHAPTER 7

Early Departures

Initially, there was hope that a passerby would stop, but the highway was barren of any vehicles, and as the night wore on, it became clear to the passengers that they would be spending an uncomfortable night in the bus. There was a half-moon that night and a myriad of stars but a thick cloud cover kept their brilliance from peeking through and all the bus driver had with him for light was an old flashlight with dead batteries. If they were to change the tire it would either have to be attempted in the dark or wait until morning.

Most of the passengers after spending some time grumbling about the actions of the bus driver finally settled in and tried to sleep. They made themselves as comfortable as possible on the worn seats either curling up, sitting up, or stretching out across the aisle. The bus driver stayed in his seat and kept the door opened just enough to let in some air, but as the desert air cooled most tried to stay warm by keeping their windows up.

Toward the back of the bus sat a married couple. The wife, a large intimidating woman named Portia, sat next to the window, which she kept open in spite of the chill. Her husband, Hiram, sat next to her. He would have preferred the window up but he had learned years ago not to ask, question, or argue with his "better half." While others tried to sleep, she continued to berate him for not doing more about their predicament.

"If you were half the man that we both know you'll never be, then you'd go out there and change the tire yourself."

Hiram looked past her toward the night sky. It would do no good to reason with her. It was easier to just agree.

"I'm sure you're right, dear."

"Of course I'm right. I don't need you to agree. Everyone here would agree if I asked them."

While Hiram took a loud and verbal beating from his beloved Portia, Susanna and Ace sat in the back of the bus quietly talking. Susanna and Ace were longtime friends and coworkers. There was a brief moment in their friendship where they wondered if it might be more, but they realized that as soon as they became serious with each they stopped getting along. They were more like siblings, so much in fact that Ace often called Susanna Sis. Ace's real name was Chester but as a newspaper reporter trying to make a name for himself in the city the name seemed dull, so he changed it to something that he thought was original and exciting. Susanna knew Ace when he was Chester and still called him that when they weren't working. She was the only one who got away with it, which was the reason they were on the bus in the first place. Ace had punched his boss in the nose after a heated argument, which had been precipitated by his boss calling him Chester.

They were on their way to an interview in a neighboring city when the bus broke down. Ace made it a habit of never showing he was nervous or worried. He saw it as a sign of weakness. Susanna knew him well enough to recognize his anxiety.

"Well, Chester," said Susanna, "I hope you get this job. I can get a job anywhere as an editor. You kind of burned your bridges back there."

"Oh, Susanna, don't you cry for me."

Susanna rolled her eyes.

"What? You used to think that was funny."

"No, I never thought it was funny. You think it's funny."

"You laughed."

"I laughed the first time you said it and that was because of the way you said it. You don't think I've heard it before? The second time you said it I smiled politely. Ever since then I've done everything I can think of to let you know how annoying it is."

Ace gave her a goofy look. She realized he was just needling her.

"Oh…you're such a jerk. Tell me what this novel is about."

"This is going to make me rich and famous, Sis. I'm telling you, it's got everything."

Susanna leaned back in the seat and closed her eyes.

"If it helps me to sleep right now, I'll buy a dozen copies. Let's hear it."

"Okay," continued Ace. "It's about The Roaring Twenties."

Without opening her eyes, Susanna yawned and said, "What are the Boring Twenties?"

"Very funny, Sis. It was a period in American history during the 1920s."

"Oh, not this again," moaned Susanna. "What is with you and American history?"

"It was such a great era. The times were big. People were giants."

"Uh-huh, well like who? By the way, I think this is working. I'm starting to get sleepy."

Ace ignored her comment and excitedly continued.

"Well, Babe Ruth, for example."

"A baby was a giant? That does sound exciting. How did that happen?"

"He wasn't a baby and stop playing around. He was a great baseball player."

Susanna made a face. "Yuck, baseball."

"The Sultan of Swat. The Big Bambino."

"Who were they?"

"The same guy silly. Those were his nicknames."

"Those are strange nicknames. Was he half Arabian and half Italian?"

Ace realized he was going to get nowhere talking about Babe Ruth.

"Never mind. He was just a great ballplayer. There were other great people in all sorts of various endeavors at the time. It's just a terrific backdrop for the story. During this time a man invents a vehicle that does everything."

"Everything?" Susanna was having almost as much fun as falling asleep.

Ace ignored her. "It rides like a motorcycle, can be converted into a car, or a boat, or even a submarine. Oh, and it can fly."

"I can't believe I'm saying this Ace, but I almost wish you would go back to talking about baseball. So what's the story?"

"Well, after he invents the thing, all the governments in the world are trying to get ahold of him and the Motorzellum."

Susanna, her eyes still closed, put her hand on Ace's arm to stop him.

"The what?"

"The Motorzellum. The vehicle he creates that changes all transportation."

"Ace, why on earth would you call it that? I mean, it transforms into different vehicles, right?"

"Yea, so?"

"Why not just call it a Transformer?"

"Transformer?" exclaimed Ace. "That just describes it. No one calls something by what it does, at least if they want to sell it and make it exciting. Transformer? That has no pizazz, no adventure." Ace laughed. "Transformer. Hah! Motorzellum, now that's a name people will remember."

"What was it called again?"

"Motorzellum."

"Oh, right. I forgot."

"Jerk."

Susanna smiled. "Bigger jerk. Okay, so he invents this thing, everyone's chasing him, trying to kill him or whatever. So what happens next?"

"A creature comes out of the sea and terrorizes all humanity."

"You're joking, right, Chester?"

"No, because now everyone needs the Motorzellum. Our man is a hero who uses the Motorzellum to save humanity."

"Well, where did this creature come from? What's his deal?"

Ace rubbed his chin. "I haven't got all the details yet. I'm thinking he used to rule earth but was driven to the depths of the sea by mankind but has decided to fight back."

"Just like that?"

Ace turned and gave Susanna a look. "Hey, like I said I haven't got all the details worked out. I'm still trying to come up with a name."

Susanna furrowed her brow and thought for a moment.

"How about Godzilla?"

"Godzilla," replied Ace. "What kind of name is that?"

"You said he kind of ran the place. So he's like a God, right? Then there's the Z thing, like the Motorzellum. They kind of go together. And the last part is like the gila monster. You know, the lizard."

Ace lifted up his hand and stuck out a forefinger.

"First of all, this ain't no religious book. So there's no God stuff. Secondly"—and as he spoke he put another finger out—"just because you don't like Motorzellum means you can give me a hard time."

Third finger out. "And last, it's just a dumb name. The gila monster doesn't go underwater. It's way too confusing and like I said, a little too religious."

Susanna laughed. "Okay, Shakespeare. Godzilla's a no-go. So what's next in this epic?"

"Well, he falls in love and..."

"Oh, why can't I fall in love?" pined Susanna. "Why can't I just meet a nice guy?"

"Um...," replied Ace undecidedly.

Susanna opened her eyes and looked up a few rows.

"See that guy up there with that loud lady who's been yelling at everyone?"

"Yea."

"Well, he's not a bad-looking fellow and he's gotta be a pretty nice guy to put up with that lip. What's he doing with her anyway?"

Ace closed his eyes while leaning back against the seat. "Okay, we're done now. You're starting to sound like an article in one of them women's mags. I'm going to sleep and see if I can dream up a better name than Godzilla."

Susanna quickly stood up and started to cut across Ace into the aisle, stepping on one of his feet.

"Ouch! Where you going?"

"That woman up there is going out for a smoke. Maybe I can bum a cigarette off her. I'm all out." Susanna moved her way toward the front of the bus and down the steps.

Hiram sat and stared straight ahead. He watched a woman walk to the front of the bus and pull out a cigarette before going outside. A moment later another woman walked past him and went outside. He knew there was nothing that could be said to his wife. He also knew that not saying anything sometimes made it worse. He decided to change the subject.

"It will be good to see your family. I'm sure your mother must have planned a big meal for us. She does make such good pies. Of course, not as good as yours dear. I think it is the crust. Yours is always a little thicker and the pie doesn't fall apart when you cut a piece. I wonder how many of your family will be there. Do you think that your cousins will show?"

Hiram turned toward Portia. She was sleeping. She made a snort and then took in a deep breath. Hiram wanted to lean over and shut the window but did not want to risk waking her. Sometimes silence was better than warmth.

Lately Hiram had been asking himself questions such as how and why he had ever married this woman. Down inside, he really knew both answers. She had bullied him into marriage just like she bullied herself into getting anything she wanted. He had married her because no else had ever shown the slightest interest in him, he was tired of living at home with his parents who constantly fought, and lastly he just did not have the will power to say no to her.

Why had she married him? Probably because no one else would have her, he reasoned. Also, and it shamed him to know this, he accepted her abuse. He was her punching bag. He was her doormat. He was her dog on the leash.

The one question that seemed to be rearing its head up more and more was would he ever do anything about it. And what to do? He had lately found himself reading news articles and obituaries that were suicide related. He found them fascinating and wondered what had propelled the people to do something so utterly drastic as taking their own life. For them, and maybe for him, life itself must have driven them to death. He did not want to die but he also did not want this life.

He had considered another possibility and that was simply to leave. She would hunt him down. He knew that. He knew that in a strange way she needed him. But it was not right. He suspected that even Portia knew that it was not right but like an addict she could not and would not stop.

He looked around and then out the window and into the night. A thought occurred to him that maybe this was the place and now was the time. He had often wondered what possible lining of the stars could produce a moment when it would be providential for him to leave. There was a peculiar feeling in the bus that anything was possible. But what would he do? He could walk down the road, hoping for a passing vehicle and get a ride. He was carrying all of the money in his wallet. Once he found a town or city, he could take a bus or a train to another city and start over. The worst that could happen would be that he could die in the desert but at least he would be going out with dignity. Dignity was something he had never known. What would it feel like to have dignity?

Hiram slid quietly off his seat and walked slowly toward the front of the bus. He held his breath, expecting any second to hear his wife call out to him, demanding what in the world he thought he was doing. Once he reached the front he slowly exhaled in relief and turned to the bus driver to open the door. The bus drivers head was turned away and Hiram could not see that his eyes were closed.

"Don't bother him," said the voice from the front seat. Hiram turned to the stranger.

"What?" answered Hiram. He had heard the stranger but he did not know what he meant.

"You can go," the stranger said. "Open the door yourself. He won't hear you. Neither will your wife. Walk for about a mile. You will find a man who's car has had a flat tire. He will give you a ride to the next town. From there, you can find transportation to wherever you choose to go. She will not find you."

Hiram stared at the stranger in disbelief. He tried to open his mouth to speak but nothing came out.

"You are being given a great gift," said the stranger. "A chance to start over. Go in peace."

Hiram turned from the stranger toward the door and noticed that it was now wide open. He haltingly went down the steps as if in a dream. Once he stepped on the ground he turned around to look back at the bus but it was gone. Hiram did as the stranger said and a mile down the road he found a man putting his jack back into the trunk.

Once off the bus, Susanna assumed the woman with a cigarette would be standing close by, next to the bus, but she was nowhere in sight.

Something is different.

The night looks new, like the first night of creation, the air feels as if it has never been breathed before, and life feels as if it is just starting. About fifteen yards ahead of the bus Susanna notices the taillights of a car.

"That's strange. Where did this come from?" Her voice seems strange to her as it falls flat into the night. There is a feeling of claustrophobia that reminds her of something that happened years ago but she can't quite put her finger on it.

Two men are standing at the car. One man has a flashlight and appears to be putting a flat tire into the trunk of his car. The other man is standing next to him.

"Hello," Susanna calls out as she nears the car. "We could use your flashlight. Our bus also has a flat tire." Both men turn to her.

"What bus?" asks the man with the flashlight.

Susanna is close enough that she sees that the other man is the man from the bus who was sitting next to the obnoxious woman.

"How did you get here?" asks Susanna. "I just walked by you on the bus."

"What bus?" repeats the man with the flashlight, this time with some irritation in his voice.

"What bus?" answers Susanna, matching the man's irritation. "That bus!"

Susanna turns to point toward the bus but all that she sees are faint road lines disappearing into blackness.

"What...what?" Susanna feels a slight pressure on her vocal cords. She fights the urge to panic. What does this remind her of?

"Did the man tell you that you could leave also?" asks Hiram.

"What? What man? Where's the bus? What is happening?"

"It is all very strange," answers Hiram. "Are you saying that you did not walk here from the bus?"

Susanna turns around and then around again.

"I just got off and you were here. How could you get here before me? What is going on?"

Then she remembers. She was a college student on vacation with school friends. They were swimming in the ocean, just off the coast. As a dare, she dove deep under some rocks. She had gotten to a point where she could not turn back and was uncertain if she could continue. For a moment there was a panic that overwhelmed her and she almost gave up. She senses that same feeling now. She just wants to find the surface and breathe.

The man with the flashlight starts to open his door and turns to Hiram and Susanna.

"Look, I'd like to get going. I'd be happy to give you a ride to the next town. I don't know anything about a bus. Do you want a ride or not?"

"Yes," answers Hiram as he opens the door to the car. "Thank you."

Both of the men turn to Susanna. The bus is gone and all she can see is the strange new night. The idea of going back seems impossible. She can barely make out the lanes in the road. The darkness seems thick and impenetrable. She can hardly take in a breath. Susanna looks at Hiram. She remembers talking about him to someone but she cannot remember who. She remembers mentioning a bus but she cannot remember why. She cannot breathe. *Do I turn back or do I go? Do I turn back to…to what? What is back there?* she asks herself. She can't remember. She can't remember anything that is back there. There is only the moment. There is no past. There is only the present and the next present. Susanna realizes she can only go forward. Just like in the water. Her body relaxes. She feels as if she had just poked her head through the surface and taken a deep breath of fresh air. She has come out the other side of something she doesn't understand and may never remember. Hiram is smiling. It is a warm and inviting smile. *He really is not a bad-looking guy*, she thinks.

"Yes, thank you for your help," said Susanna as she slid into the car.

Surprisingly the bus driver had fallen asleep quickly. The combination of what he had seen in the road and the inconvenience, not to mention the danger, that he had put the passengers through overwhelmed him and he fell into a deep sleep.

He dreamed he was in church. The pastor was speaking and the dream felt so real that the bus driver thought that the dream was the reality and the reality of what had happened on the bus had been a bad dream. He sighed and smiled. The relief in feeling that what had happened on the bus was not real flowed through him. The pastor was preaching on the verse in Revelation, "The dead in Christ shall rise first." He thought of his father. As he did he felt his mother's fingers rest on his hand. The pastor's voice continued, "And in 1 Thessalonians 4:17, 'We who are still alive and are left shall be caught up.'" The bus driver squeezed his mother's hand. "We who are still alive and are left," the pastor repeated. Then again, "We who are still alive and are left." Then again and again it was repeated like a record skipping. The bus driver, puzzled, looked toward the pulpit. The dead man in the brown suit silently stared back at him from the pulpit. He turned his head to look into his mother's face but she seemed not to notice. She looked back at him with a quizzical look— the kind she had given him in the past when she knew something was bothering him. The pastor's voice continued in a flat tone, "There is nothing hidden that shall not be made known."

The bus driver buried his head in his hands. *Wake up, wake up, wake up*, he told himself. Verses kept flowing from the pulpit, "Whosoever conceals his transgression shall not prosper," "Woe to the rebellious children who execute a plan but not mine," "The secret things belong to the Lord." The bus driver shook his head back and forth crying out, "No, no, no." The verses stopped but he could hear words ringing through the church. "Conceal, judge, secret, hidden…" repeating over and over again. He stood and turned toward his mother who was no longer there. It was the man. The whole church was filled with the image of the man in the brown suit. This was more than a dream. It was more than a nightmare. He hoped it wasn't reality but it certainly felt real. He ran wildly past the figures of men staring silently at him toward the exit doors of the church. There were two of the figures at the door standing on either side. The bus driver closed his eyes, lowered his head, and drove his shoulder into the double doors, flinging himself outside.

He found himself engulfed in a brilliant light. He could hear a faint humming which he could not define but which was quite pleasant. He started to relax. There was a faint yellow hue in the distance and he wondered what it could be. He thought he might walk toward it when he felt a hand rest on his shoulder. When he turned around he saw the man in the brown suit.

He opened his eyes and gasped like someone who had been underwater too long and had finally come up for air. It was early morning and the sun was blasting through the bus window. He was drenched in sweat but not sweat from the heat. The air was still cool. He ran his fingers through his hair, slicking it back from his forehead. He kept a jacket to his left which he had taken off the night before and picked it up, wiping his face with it. His hands were gripped onto the top of the steering wheel and he rested his head on them, taking deep breaths and brushing away the nasty cobwebs of his nightmare. Some snoring from the back of the bus reminded him that they would soon be expecting him to get out and fix the tire. He turned around stiffly and looked at the passengers. *The sooner the better*, he thought to himself as he slowly started to get up and exit the bus.

"I wouldn't do that," a voice said.

The bus driver, startled to hear a voice, did a slight jump.

"Whoa, what?"

"I would not go outside if I were you," said the voice again.

It was one of the passengers in the front seat across from the bus driver. He had been sitting in the seat with his legs stretched out toward the isle and sat up as the bus driver had started to reach for the door. He was a man in his late twenties with dark hair and a tattoo on his forearm which had three vertical bars intersecting with two horizontal bars. He had light blue eyes which at the moment presented a fierce seriousness.

"What are you talking about?" asked the bus driver.

"If you leave the bus now, you will not come back."

The bus driver smiled. "Don't worry. I'm not going anywhere. I'm just going to see how bad the tire is and if it can be fixed. I might need your help if it can."

"That's not what I mean. Did you have a passenger count when you left?"

"No," answered the bus driver. "I don't work with a passenger log. Why?"

"Because some of your passengers are gone and by gone, I don't mean they've wandered off."

The bus driver looked perplexed, annoyed, and weary at the same time. "I don't know what you're talking about. Excuse me Mr...," the bus driver paused as he grabbed the door.

The man grabbed the driver's arm hard. It occurred to the bus driver that the stranger's grip on his arm was such that if the stranger had wanted to he could hold that arm as long as he felt necessary. There seemed to be no sense of effort on the stranger's part.

"Ward. You can call me Mr. Ward if that helps. Look, it doesn't matter to me if you live or die, but you're the bus driver and I'm not sure if we can change this tire or continue on without you, so I'm telling you, don't go outside or something very unexpected will happen. I've been watching people leave the bus and as soon as they touch the ground, they disappear."

The bus driver stared at the stranger and at first wanted to laugh, partly because it was the last thing he expected to hear and partly because it just sounded silly, like something an imaginative child might say to an adult. There was however nothing childish or silly about Mr. Ward. If what he said was true then it would make sense to tell someone no matter how crazy it sounded. He thought of his dream. A chill went through body. As absurd as it sounded, there was something about the man that made the bus driver think he knew more than he was saying.

"If others are disappearing as you say, then why haven't you stopped them?"

The man released his grip and leaned back in the seat.

"Well, first of all, as I mentioned, I don't really care if people want to leave or not. Most of them are free to decide. But you're the bus driver. Secondly, I thought you could use the rest. Did you have a good sleep?"

The stranger spoke as if he already knew the answer but he did not give the bus driver an opportunity to respond.

"I've seen two people leave. Not to mention that woman who went out last night for a cigarette. I don't see her. And her kid, the mute with the chalkboard, was worried enough last night to get up the nerve to try and look for her. She, I did stop from going out." The stranger smiled broadly. "For the moment it helps that she is a little afraid of me."

The bus driver rubbed his chin and sat back down. Some of the passengers were starting to wake up. Some were looking at him, and he sensed that they were expecting him to fix the tire and get them going again. A service man in uniform stood and started walking toward the front of the bus. He had a friendly, yet serious manner about him. As he approached the front of the bus, the stranger nodded at the bus driver.

"Watch," he said.

The soldier took the last few steps and turned toward the bus driver as if he were turning on a military march. The bus driver almost expected to be saluted but instead he heard the firm voice of the soldier.

"Sir, would you like some help with the tire?"

The bus driver stood. The stranger lifted his hand slightly, just enough to get the soldiers' attention.

"We're right behind you soldier. Thank you for your service," said the stranger politely.

The soldier turned to the stranger and gave him a look, which clearly represented his disdain and confusion that the stranger was even speaking to him, much less not already outside helping the bus driver change the tire. The stranger smiled back. The soldier turned back toward the bus driver who smiled weakly.

"He's Mr. Ward," said the bus driver.

"I see," answered the bus driver. "Well, I'll be outside when you are ready."

With that, he turned toward the door as sharply as before. As soon as the soldier touched his feet to the ground he was gone. The bus driver's jaw dropped as if he had just seen a magic trick performed by the stranger. He kept staring out the bus waiting for the soldier to reappear so that everyone could applaud. He turned toward the stranger stunned and with a questioning look. The stranger smiled again as if he too had seen a magic trick, only he seemed less surprised and more appreciative of what had just happened.

Only a few groggy passengers saw what had happened and because of their view they were not quite certain the soldier was gone, but possibly just out of their sight. Enough of a commotion was caused so that more people were now awake and sitting up, including one heavy set woman whose head was rotating back and forth as if on a swivel. Her interest was not on the soldier but on the whereabouts of her husband. She turned clumsily around and looked back at the bathroom door on the bus. A woman was just coming out. The heavy set woman slid away from the window toward the aisle and stood up roughly. She was breathing heavily, partly from her size but mostly because she was angry. Anyone who had ever casually been acquainted with her knew her as the angry woman they tried to avoid if possible. The previous night she had been one of the loudest complainers and by the time people settled down to sleep she was even more disliked than the bus driver. The angry woman stood up and stomped to the front of the bus, shouting out as she went.

"Hiram, where have you run off too? Hiram!"

She gave the bus driver a nasty snarl as she walked by him and turned to leave the bus.

"Don't go out," said the bus driver weekly.

Ignoring the bus driver, the woman said loudly to no in particular, "Where's my husband? I don't seem him anywhere."

"I believe he left earlier," answered Mr. Ward. The bus driver rolled his eyes at the stranger who just grinned back.

"Please do not go out," repeated the bus driver. By now most of the passengers were up and were either watching the exchange between the bus driver and the woman or looking outside.

Portia gave a snort, forcefully grabbed the door and opened it. Before the bus driver could speak or try to stop her, she stormed off the bus and planted her feet firmly on the ground. There was a large gasp from those watching as she disappeared.

CHAPTER 8

The Motorzellum

Ace awoke in the middle of the night with a start. He was lying on his back with his legs dangling over the seat. For a moment, he couldn't remember where he was or how long he had slept. He couldn't tell if it was a few hours or a few days. He felt completely disoriented as he sat up and looked around. There was a painful crick in his neck that he tried to massage.

There was a man in overalls sitting in the seat across from Ace. He did not remember seeing the man earlier. With the exception of the man in overalls there appeared to be only one other person on the bus, a man sitting at the front of the bus near the door.

Ace stood up and faced the man in the overalls. The man was looking straight ahead with his eyes open. He had no eyelids. Being in darkness the man's pasty white skin stood out.

"Hey," said Ace. "Where'd everyone go?"

The man in the overalls sat still. Eventually his face slowly turned toward Ace but his eyes never met Ace's look. It was as if the man had heard a noise but did seem to comprehend someone had spoken to him. Without speaking, the man gradually moved his head back and Ace felt the hairs on the back of his neck stand up. Ace stepped cautiously into the aisle, past the man, and headed toward the front.

He passed one empty seat after another, looking through the windows into the black night wondering where in the world everyone went. About halfway up he noticed a small girl asleep on one of the seats. She had a small chalkboard that was tucked partially under one of her arms. There was some writing on it. He could only make out one word, "help," but unless he pulled the chalkboard away from her, he could not read the rest. He thought of trying to wake her but he had an eerie notion that he shouldn't, or that if he tried, he would be unsuccessful. The bus had such a strange feel to it, he thought. How did everything change so much and where in the world was everybody?

He walked toward the one other person sitting at the front near the door. He was a young man with his feet up on the rail in front. The bus driver was gone also. Perhaps he was changing the tire and everyone else was outside watching him. That didn't make sense to Ace, but nothing seemed to make sense. Perhaps the stranger could explain everything. If not, Ace had decided he was going to leave anyway. He was not going to sit around in this tin can any longer with that creep in the back and the mystery girl sleeping.

"Excuse me, do you know what is happening?" asked Ace of the stranger.

The man turned toward Ace and smiled slightly. He lacked the sinister horror of the man at the back of the bus but there was still an unexplainable strangeness to him which was equally frightening.

"Yes, Chester, I do," answered the man.

Normally Chester would have demanded that the stranger not only tell him how he knew his name but that he call him Ace or else the man would wish he had never been born. But nothing was as it should be and Chester was on unsteady ground.

"Where is everyone? Where is Susanna?"

"Everyone is where they should be Chester, doing what they should be doing. What do you think you should be doing now? Where do you think you should be?"

Chester was taken back by the questions. He felt as if her were on trial being asked to explain his life. He wanted to step off the bus, but oddly felt that he could not until the man gave him his permission.

"I... I guess I should be somewhere getting a job," answered Chester as truthfully as he could. "I'm a reporter. That's what I do."

The stranger smiled.

"Um...yes, Chester, a reporter. Chester, do you believe in time travel?"

"Um,..."

"Well, it doesn't exist," declared the stranger. "Well, not the way people think. People look at time as linear. Past, present, future, so on. And those obviously exist but time itself is not a solid line, at least not unless it needs to be. Are you following me, Chester?"

Chester started to speak but couldn't quite figure what words to use. The stranger continued.

"You see, Chester, time is like a metal. Think of a steel beam. It has a certain weight, a certain length, a certain width. It can be measured and it can have a purpose. That's how people see time. But what if we melt the metal and reshape it. It no longer follows the direction or path of its prior appearance. Time is like that. One doesn't travel through time like it's some kind of two way tunnel. Time is reshaped and settles on a different experience in reality. That's why you are here right now on the bus with everyone gone. The person who believes in time travel in its traditional sense would say that you have gone a few days into the future but that's just not how it works. I've often wondered if this is how the Master knows everything. It's not that He has travelled back and forth but that he shapes time to a reality. At least that's what I think. What do you think, Chester?"

"Ah... I don't know," stammered Chester.

The stranger laughed. There was no sense of mocking. It was a warm and genuine laugh.

"Good answer, Chester. I can see why you are going to write about it."

"Write about what?" asked Chester.

"The Motorzellum," said the stranger.

The color drained from Chester's face.

"Who are you?" he asked, unable to mask the fear he felt.

"You know, Chester, I think you should write the novel. It will save the world and it will also change your life. It won't be entirely pleasant but in the end you will have great contentment, which is something that you lack. You know what else? I think you should write it under the name Ace. I know it's a little vain but I like it. What do you think... Ace?"

"What...what?" stuttered Chester.

The stranger swept his hand through the air as if he was displaying a large billboard.

"Ace Field, the famous novelist."

Ace stared dumbly at the stranger.

"That's right, Chester. I know why you don't like, Chester. Chester Field. It's so silly to be bothered by that, don't you think, Chester? But do you know what you need, Chester?" said the stranger rubbing his chin.

Chester made an inarticulate sound, somewhere between a guttural grunt and a high squeak. The stranger continued.

"I think you need some inspiration. They say a truly great writer must be inspired. There's no doubt you have ideas Ace, but you lack spark. You lack..." The young man paused in joyful fun, something which Ace was unable to appreciate at the moment. A broad smile came across the young man's face. The bus for a moment seemed to light up.

"You need...pizazz."

Ace started to speak but the stranger lifted his hand, motioning for Ace to stop.

"Look," said the stranger as he nodded toward the front of the bus. The bus headlights suddenly came on and in front of the bus stood the Motorzellum.

Ace forgot all the strangeness that had just happened since he awoke. All he saw was the Motorzellum. The fact that one had never existed except vaguely in his imagination did not disturb him at all. He never realized until that moment how important it was to him. It also did not seem to bother him that he knew it instinctively to be the Motorzellum. He just knew it was and that he must have it.

"Can I?" asked Ace.

"Ride it and write about it," said the stranger. "It will raise you up and it will ruin you, but in the end it will lead you to salvation."

Ace was barely listening as he walked off the bus and approached the Motorzellum. In its motorcycle state it was long, wide, and black as the night. Ace lifted his leg reverently over the seat and placed both hands carefully but firmly on the handlebars. He looked down at the gauges in front of him. There were five simple buttons in gold, clearly marked as Water, Air, Bike, Car, and Tank. Below that was a silver switch marked on/off. Chester flipped the "on" switch and revved up the engine. He turned around and gave the stranger a thumbs-up before riding off into the desert.

Ace rode like the wind through the desert night, his high beams lighting up the desert road. The bike was incredibly light, which was surprising for its size. Ace could not figure out what the metal was but it possessed the lightness of aluminum yet at the same time felt as solid as a lead pipe. After some time of riding, he hit the switch for car and the Motorzellum transformed into a solid four-door limousine.

The transformation was not the type that Ace was expecting. He had never really thought the process through but he had imagined the possibility that invisible panels would open up somewhere on the bike and envelope it. However, as he rode, the metal began to melt. There was no heat and somehow the bike managed to keep him seated while it molded itself into the shape of the limousine. Ace thought of the strangers comment about time being like a metal that melts and reshapes itself. Maybe many unexplainable things were linked to this truth. As he cruised up and down the desert highway, Ace realized that he would never figure out the how's and why's in which the Motorzellum had become a limousine. As the Motorzellum transformed, it brought up a new panel, which had additional features. There were various shield features and weapons along with an invisibility function.

Ace rode, flew, and sailed the Motorzellum, which not only could ride on the surface of the water, but also transformed into a submarine. He circled the globe, explored the deepest sea, and traversed the highest mountain peaks. He found the Motorzellum could not only fly but also could change into a rocket ship. He flew the Motorzellum higher and higher through the atmosphere and toward the sun. He had never felt so free and invincible.

Three days later, Ace was found on the side of the desert highway, face up on the ground staring at the sun with an adventurous yet raw skin grin. Had anyone followed him around for the last few days they would have seen a man out of his mind running crazily around the desert, pretending at times to be riding a motorcycle or mimicking someone flying a plane. He was barely alive when a passerby stopped to pick him up and take him to a hospital. Ace was in and out of consciousness for weeks, at times mumbling incoherently and other times screaming out deliriously.

It took eight weeks for Ace's wounds to heal and as they did he gradually slipped into a deep depression. It had all seemed so real. There were times when he could feel the vibration of the motorcycle as if he were still speeding down the highway. He had tried once to explain everything to a doctor only to see from the doctor's reaction that not only would no one ever believe him but that if he persisted in talking about it they might put him in a straitjacket and throw away the key.

After being released from the hospital, Ace went back to writing but his heart was not in it. His stories for the paper lacked any kind of spark and it wasn't long before the only work he could get was writing obituaries. As the weeks turned into months, Ace wrote obituaries, drank, aimlessly walked the streets, and occasionally got into bar fights. He wandered his way through the spring, summer, and fall and by Christmas he had stopped haunting the bars and just drank alone in his apartment while trying to earn just enough money to pay the rent and buy something to drink.

One night, while walking out of the liquor store he saw a drunk laying in the gutter. His voice was barely understandable but the melody was not.

"Oh, Susanna, don't you cry for me," the drunk bellowed out. He botched the following words, "Oh banjo Alabama and I need a knee," then started laughing hysterically which eventually turned into a painfully drawn out hacking cough. Ace walked toward the man and as he did so, the drunk looked up at Ace through glazed wandering eyes.

"Hey, sailor," slurred the drunk. "Buy a gal a drink?" The drunk laughed uproariously again.

Susanna. How could I have forgotten about her? Ace thought. Somehow he had remembered everything so clearly yet forgotten about Susanna. He looked down at the bottle in his hand.

"Here you go, friend," said Ace as he handed the bottle to the drunk. The drunk took a large gulp and handed the bottle back to Ace while burping out a thank-you.

"No," said Ace. "You keep it."

The drunk tried to sound sober while talking.

"To what do I owe this great honor, your honor?"

"You reminded me of an old friend and what she thought of me. You reminded me of what I am."

Ace walked away and could hear the man cry out, "to old friends and why they're mean, I mean where they've been, or something. Haha!"

Five weeks later, Ace finished his novel. Rejected by the major publishing firms Ace was finally able to get it published by an obscure paperback publisher who was only able to offer him a percentage based on sales. He published a test run of two hundred books. The book sold for $1.25. One hundred and eleven copies in total were bought. Ace made $13.88. The test run had ended after the first lap.

The remaining eighty-nine books were stored away in a ware-house with other failures that the publisher had managed to accumu-late. They sat there for a few years gathering dust and then one day the entire lot of eighty-nine books was bought by a foreigner who had showed up at the publishers house asking specifically for Ace's book.

Three months later, Ace was walking down Central Avenue. He had worked his way back as a reporter for the local paper and though his book had never become the success he thought it was going to be, he had made peace with the peculiar events he had experienced and moved on. It had been a tough year, he thought to himself, but he had come through it a wiser and better man. He turned the corner and walked down an empty alley he used as a short cut back to the office. It was then that he discovered things were about to get much worse than anything he had previously experienced. A van pulled up next to him, screeched to a halt, and before he could do anything, three men jumped out, grabbed him, threw him into the van and sped off.

While two of the men held him down the third pushed a needle into Ace's arm. While Ace slept his captors drove to a warehouse where he was packaged in a large crate and shipped in a private plane to a small county. He awoke fourteen hours later in a small damp cell, still in his box but the lid off. He sat up stiffly and looked around. There were two beds with one of them occupied by a toothless, old blind man in rags, whom Ace would soon discover also happened to be deaf.

Ace tried to find some way to communicate with the man and see if he could learn anything about where he was but all the man did was draw some strange squiggles on the grimy cement floor which made no sense. While Ace was pondering the squiggles, he heard some voices outside his cell. He jumped up and ran to the metal door and began to pound.

"Hey, what am I doing here? Let me out!"

After a moment he could hear someone on the other side put his key in the keyhole and turn the handle. The door opened and two men in green fatigues stood facing Ace. One of the guards had his gun drawn at the doorway while the other marched in, pushing Ace roughly to the ground. The old man found his way to one corner and whimpered.

"Hey," snapped Ace at the guard as he barged past. The guard ignored Ace and headed to the container Ace had been delivered in. The guard grabbed the side of the case and picked it up easily and walked back to the door. Within seconds, he was gone and the door slammed shut.

"Hey," yelled Ace again. He looked over at the old man crouched down in the corner and then back to the door.

"Idiots," he muttered.

For three days, Ace sat and slept in the small cell with the old man. It was impossible to communicate with the man, whose abilities were limited to some incomprehensible sounds and random drawings on the floor. Food was given to him twice a day and consisted of potatoes and stale bread. Screaming out had no effect on his captors much less the old man. Ace was at his wits end by the end of the third day when suddenly a door opened and two men came in, grabbed Ace roughly under each arm and dragged him silently to another room. They slammed him into a metal chair in the middle of the room and pointed a bright light at his face. Ace could see nothing with the light directly in his eyes but quickly felt the stale breath of a man inches away from his face just before the man screamed.

"Tell us how you discovered the Motorzellum."

"What?" answered Ace.

"The Motorzellum, you idiot, the Motorzellum. What a stupid name you have called it. How did you come by its design?"

"Who are you?" demanded Ace. "I can't make out your accent." Ace paused a moment. "Are you Nazis?"

"Hah," answered the man with the stale breath. "The Nazi's wish they were us. That's how bad we are."

Ace could hear others in the room murmuring their approval of what their beloved Commander Stale Breath was saying. Ace couldn't figure out who these clowns were and what they were all about. If he hadn't spent the last three days in a prison cell he would have thought the whole thing was an elaborate practical joke.

"It is no concern to you who we are, but I can tell you that we make Nazi's look like Sunday school children. Now tell us about the bike or we slowly start torturing you until you do. How did you steal our secret?"

Ace laughed and one of the other men from the back room strode toward Ace and slapped him hard against the face. Ace fell over onto the floor.

"Sit up," ordered Commander Stale Breath. Ace climbed back in the chair.

"Thinking this is amusing will not help you."

Ace rubbed his jaw. "I'm laughing because you will never believe me if I tell you the truth and no matter how much you torture me I don't know enough to make up a lie. I am laughing because it is absurd and frightening at the same time."

The man leaned in closer. "Good. You should be frightened and you should not presume what I will or will not believe." The man leaned in so close that Ace thought he might be ill from the man's breath. Ace recognized the stale smell as asparagus. "Now tell me your absurd tale and I will decide what to believe."

So Ace shrugged his should and told him about his time on the bus, the stranger, and his imaginary ride on the Motorzellum which led to the writing of his novel.

"In the end," Ace concluded with a sigh, "it was just a story I made up that nobody wanted to read."

There was a long silence as Ace sat in the chair, looking downward to keep his eyes out of the light. After some time he could hear the door open and a number of people leaving. Though Ace could not see the leader, he knew from his heavy breathing that the leader was somewhere still in the room watching him. Eventually a voice came from one of the corners.

"That has to be one of the strangest, stupidest, most unbelievable stories I have ever heard." The man walked toward Ace and leaned in, his mouth next to Ace's ear.

"The old man is dead. You will have the cell to you alone to give you time to come up with another story, hopefully for you not so foolish. I am still looking into you and who you are. Either way you will not be leaving for a while."

"Have you really invented the Motorzellum?" asked Ace.

The man stood and walked toward the door. He called out something Ace did not understand. He could hear footsteps from the other side of the door approaching. The man turned to Ace just before leaving.

"Motorzellum. Such an idiotic name."

As the man with the stale breath left and two guards came in, Ace muttered, "Susanna wasn't too crazy about it either."

Ace was thrown into his cell, now made empty by the death of the old man. In spite of the fact that it was nearly impossible to develop any kind of friendship with the old man Ace found he missed him. Days passed into weeks while Ace was left alone. Ace was unaware that while he languished alone in his cell, Commander

Stale Breath was doing everything he could to verify Ace's story and coming up empty. But others were also looking into Ace such as Susanna, who had bought one of the few copies of Ace's book and had been trying to contact him. When she discovered that Ace had gone missing, she asked her husband Hiram, who worked for the State Department, to see what could be found out about Ace's disappearance. At first Hiram thought that it was a local matter for the police to investigate but when he discovered a witness who saw Ace thrown into a van he started to ask around. There had been rumors that a scientist had developed a vehicle which used a technology far beyond anything anyone had ever imagined. Hiram had known about Ace's book but never bothered to read it. He was surprised to find the description of what Ace called the Motorzellum extremely detailed and matched many of the early rumored reports of the scientist developments. In time, Hiram became convinced that not only had Ace been kidnapped by the people who were building the bike but that they intended to use the bike against them. A team was set in motion not only to free Ace but to destroy or prevent the making of the Motorzellum.

Six days later, a select team of operatives invaded the compound where they discovered the scientist murdered, plans for the Motorzellum destroyed, and a handful of prisoners, including Ace.

Ace was flown home where he met with Susanna and her husband Hiram.

"So where have you been hiding?" teased Ace.

"I have not been hiding. If anyone disappeared it was you Chester. By the way, you look awful." Susanna slipped her arm around Hiram's. "This is Hiram my husband." Hiram reached out and shook his hand.

"It's a pleasure to meet you Chester...er, Ace. I'm not sure which to call you. Susanna always refers to you as Chester but told me you prefer Ace."

"It doesn't really matter anymore Hiram. Your call."

Susanna raised an eyebrow. "Really?"

Chester shrugged his shoulders. "Yeah, sis, really. I'm so glad to be out, you can call me Peter Pan for all I care."

Chester turned toward Hiram.

"So, Hiram, I understand you got me out. I can't tell you how grateful I am. I owe you."

Susanna raised her eyebrow again. "Really?"

"All right sis, that'll do. So anyway, Hiram, what's this all about?"

"Well, ah Chester. It seems you somehow managed to uncover something that was being developed by a madman who had intended it to cause great harm to as many people as possible. I don't know how you did it but if you had not written that novel we probably would not have gone after him until it was too late."

Chester shrugged his shoulders again and Susanna laughed.

"I can't believe that stupid little idea brought this all about," said Susanna.

"Jerk," answered Ace.

"Bigger jerk," replied Susanna.

"Unfortunately," continued Hiram, "somehow this has leaked to the press. I'm afraid that you are going to be pestered by reporters."

Susanna laughed again. "That is so perfect."

"I'll be right back, my dear," said Hiram. "I have to brief the council. Ace, you are as interesting as Susanna has told me. Best of luck to you." With that, Hiram gave Susanna a kiss on the cheek and squeezed her hand before leaving.

Chester sighed. "Such as nice guy."

"Shut up, Chester. He is."

"I know, Susanna. I'm happy for you. How did you hook that fish anyway?"

"I don't know if it was so much me hooking him," answered Susanna. "We both just sort of fell into the same net. How much do you remember about that bus ride?"

Chester told his tale of waking up, the empty bus, the stranger, and his bizarre journey after that. He told her how he had remembered everything but her until he met the drunk man singing that song.

"You know, it's funny, Chester. For quite a while, I could not remember anything. Hiram was very patient with me. Then slowly pieces of my life came back. The only part I couldn't remember was you. How could we work so long together and I don't remember you? Then one day I was at a church fair and I saw your book on a table and everything about you came back."

"Boy, was that whole thing odd," said Chester.

"You should write a book about it, Chester. You would have no problem now that you're a big deal."

"I don't want to be a big deal anymore," answered Chester.

But Chester Field, a.k.a. Ace Field, did become a big deal. Everyone learned that his novel had helped the government stop a nation from attacking the world. Ace's book was republished and sold more copies than Ace could dream of. Finding fame not as enticing as he once thought, Ace Field retired and moved to a secluded island where he met a missionary named Jenny Flubb. Much to his surprise Chester became "religious," though he realized that what he had once thought was religious, was in fact truth, simple and powerful. A few years later, Chester and Jenny were married. Chester spent the remaining years of his life happily serving on the mission field with his beloved Jenny.

CHAPTER 9

Henri

It was around two in the morning when Henri awoke with a night-mare. In the dream he had been at a friend's house playing in his room. His friend had called Henri over to his window to look at an old woman, bent over while she clutched a cane walking down the street. Henri pulled the curtains back just enough for one eye to peek between the crack in the curtains. As he did so the old woman stopped, and without moving the rest of her body, slowly turned her head to Henri and looked right at him. Her face was hideous. In the dream Henri had jumped back, away from the curtain. In his sleep he also jumped, which caused him to awaken. Everywhere he looked in his room he had that awful feeling that every dark corner hid the frightening woman of his nightmare. He got out of bed and sought his mother's room.

His mother's room was down the hallway, but Henri could see that a light was on downstairs and he could hear muffled voices. His thought was to go down stairs but as he reached the top of the stairs he decided instead to listen in on the conversation.

"So it hurts right now?" Henri recognized the voice of his moth-er's friend Mrs. Champli. She lived in the apartment down the hall. Ever since he could remember she had babysat for Henri whenever his mother had to work.

"Oh, yes, Eve. It always hurts," answered Henri's mother.

"Well, what did the doctor say, Molly?" asked Eve.

Molly started to speak but Eve interrupted.

"Henri is asleep, isn't he, Molly?"

"Yes, Eve, he won't hear. But what I am going to tell you I will have to tell Henri tomorrow. I will not keep any more secrets from him."

Henri leaned his head in, hoping that no one would hear him. He had completely forgotten about his nightmare.

"But, Molly. You had to keep what happened to his father from him. Don't blame yourself for that. How could you tell him what you don't know?"

"You know, Eve, it's been over ten years and every day I still expect, or maybe just hope, that Auberon is going to walk through that door with his beautiful, dopey grin and have a perfectly good reason why he left. It just wasn't like him to disappear like that, especially the day Henri was born. Which is why I have always told Henri that his father died in a car accident. It's as good a reason as any. I just can't imagine it being anything that Auberon would have done on purpose."

"You still don't have a detective looking for him, do you?" asked Eve.

"No, no. I stopped that long ago. It was a waste of money. What are they going to do? I was hoping they would find his car and that might answer some questions, but they never found anything."

Molly pressed her fingers to her temple and tried to massage her head.

"I'm sorry, Molly. That's none of my business. Do you want to talk tomorrow? You look tired, dear."

"No, Eve, I need to tell you about the doctor. It's bad. Much worse than he thought." Molly looked at Eve and tried unsuccessfully to keep the tears from falling. As she spoke she realized it was the first time she was going to say the words out loud. Up until this moment it had not seemed real. Tears started rolling down her cheeks as she spoke.

"There's something wrong with my brain. Some kind of tumor or something like that. The doctor says I have less than a year. It can be anywhere from a few months to about a year. He told me that when the headaches become unbearable it will only be a matter of weeks, if not days. When that happens I will have to check into the hospital until the end."

Molly sat still, staring straight at her best friend Eve, who was frozen and pale, tears falling down her cheeks and onto the table. Then she slid her chair over to her friend and they sobbed together as quietly as they could. Suddenly there was a thud from upstairs. Henri had fainted.

Henri didn't know he had fainted. The last thing he remembered was that he felt nauseous and his head had started to spin. He had closed his eyes and when he opened them he was standing in a desert on the side of a road. Henri turned around and all that was visible was a flat, desolate sea of desert. The physical sensations he felt went beyond that of a dream. It was a hot summer day and the heat beat down on his back. He could also feel the heat of the ground rising through his shoes. Henri did not feel a sense of strangeness or panic. For some reason, it seemed familiar even though he had never been to the desert. Henri looked to his left and thought he could see off in the distance the faint outline of a small building. As he was trying to figure out what the building might be and whether he should head toward it he heard a sound to his right and looked up the road. There appeared on the horizon a small dot which grew larger as it approached him. As it drew nearer he realized it was a bus. He almost expected it to stop but instead it flew past him. He could see passengers in the bus. A blur of faces raced by, but one face, that of a young girl was staring at him. Time and the bus seemed to pause as their eyes met. Henri's eyes followed the girl's gaze down the road as the bus passed him.

When the bus was out of sight, Henri turned his head back and saw that across the road a man was facing him, standing there just as if the bus had dropped him off. He was standing in front of a car. Henri could see that the back tire was flat. The man was smiling at Henri. Even though Henri only knew his father from pictures, he recognized immediately that it was him.

"Father," cried Henri as he started to cross the street. Auberon lifted his hand toward Henri to stop. He then pointed toward the road between them. Henry looked down at the road and noticed that the road had become a gulf between them as if they were standing on opposite sides of cliffs. He looked back toward his father with a feeling of desperation but his father was gone. The desert was gone. He was engulfed in whiteness.

"Henri? Henri?" a voice said.

Henri opened his eyes. A man was standing over him, shining a bright light into his eyes. Henri could see his mother behind him.

"There we go. Welcome back Henri. How are you feeling? You have a nasty bump on your head."

Molly went around the doctor and knelt by Henri's side, taking one of his hands.

"Are you okay, dear?"

"Yea, Mom. What happened?"

"You must have passed out. You were at the top of the stairs and I heard a loud bang. I called Dr. Benson over. Is he all right, Doctor?"

"Yes, he's gonna be fine. Just a bump on the head."

The doctor performed some simple tests on Henri and then had him sit up to see if he was dizzy.

"Mom, I saw Dad," Henri said excitedly.

The doctor looked questionably at Molly.

"Thank you, Doctor," Molly said quickly. "If you think he's going to be all right then why don't we go downstairs and I can pay you for your trouble. It was so kind of you to hurry over."

"Nonsense, Molly. I'm just a floor above you."

Molly started toward the door with the doctor following.

"Henri, why don't you rest a bit and I'll be up shortly."

By the time Molly returned Henri had fallen asleep. At first she was worried that he might have passed out but as she came closer she could see that he was breathing. She pulled his covers over him and brushed back his hair, looking into his face. *How much had he heard?* she wondered.

The next morning, Henri awoke as if nothing had happened. He commented on the bump on his head but said nothing about his father or the conversation he had overheard. Molly wasn't sure if Henri had decided not to talk about what he had heard or if Henri really did not remember. Since Henri had not mentioned his father again she decided against bringing it up. One thing she could not avoid was letting Henri know she did not have long to live. Four months later she was gone and Henri found himself on a bus stuck in the desert.

In spite of the passengers being annoyed by the flat tire and a night spent in an uncomfortable bus, Henri could not help but feel a rush of excitement and adventure. He had been travelling with his uncle by bus for nearly two days now and with the exception of smiling at the girl in the row near him it had been a tedious journey.

The uncle was very nice but it was an awkward ride for both of them. The uncle was not sure how to comfort Henri and Henri was not sure how to be comforted. As a young boy he had never learned how to live with a father and now he would have to learn to live without a mother. He was too young to know how sorry he should feel for himself. He knew he was sad. He tried to not think too much of his mother around other people because it made him cry and he did not want others to see that. He was a little nervous about where he would be going and what it would be like but he didn't know enough to be discouraged or even worried. So like most boys, Henri spent most of the time staring out of the window looking at the few desert sites they passed, hoping he could see something interesting.

The night the bus broke down, Henri had hoped that he would be able to go outside and explore, especially when he heard that a dog was hit by the bus. But amidst the complaining and arguing, which Henri also found fascinating to watch, his uncle told him that it was best to stay inside and try to get some sleep. Henri didn't know his uncle well enough to plead his case so he continued to watch the passengers and look outside the best he could to see if there were any adventures he might be missing. Eventually, the passengers started to calm down as well as Henri's curiosity so he leaned his head on the window against the make-shift pillow made from his uncle's jacket and tried to sleep. He was just starting to nod off when he heard someone softly crying. It was the girl. He noticed that the mother was not with her and remembered that it was some time ago that he had seen her go outside with a cigarette in her hand.

It was quiet in the bus except for some snoring and Henri tip-toed past his sleeping uncle and hunched his way over to the girl and sat beside her. She looked up with a short start. Henri could tell that the girl first looked excited at the prospect that her mother might have returned and then saw her face turn to a brief disappointment mixed with fear and maybe a little happiness at seeing him.

"Are you all right?" Henri whispered.

Elena shook her head no.

"Where is your mother? Didn't she ever come back?"

Elena shook her head no again and looked out the window, almost hoping that by talking about her, it might bring her back.

"Do you want me to go look for her?" Henri felt very gallant asking this question even though the prospect of going out in the middle of the desert night seemed a little too much for him.

Elena wrote on her board that the man up front would not let her, only to save space, she just wrote "man said no." She nodded to the man sitting near the door of the bus.

Henri squinted to read the writing. In spite of the white chalk it was still difficult to read. He stared intently at the man and contemplated going up and demand that he be allowed to go out and look for the mother. But that also seemed a little too daunting. After a moment, he turned to Elena and asked her name. She wrote it on the chalkboard.

"I'm Henri," he whispered. The girl smiled.

Henri sat with her the rest of the night. It seemed to help her to not worry about her mother and Henri enjoyed being with someone his own age. At one point his uncle had awakened and noticed Henri sitting with the girl. He gave Henri a nod to indicate that it was okay for him to stay there.

In the morning Henri awoke first. Elena was lying down curled up on his lap, her chalkboard lying on the floor just under the seat in front of them. Henri thought of trying to pick it up but he did not want to disturb Elena. He was getting sore from sitting so long and he wanted to stretch his legs. He did the best he could by extending his feet and twisting them around to try and stretch them. That is when the large woman came past him heading up to the front of the bus.

The conversation from the woman and the bus driver drifted back and woke Elena. She sat up and smiled shyly at Henri and then gave him a questioning look about the woman up front. Henri shrugged his shoulders to indicate he did not know, but he did notice that a number of people had gone to windows on the door side. Henri stood and swiftly crossed the aisle to an empty seat. Kneeling on the seat, he opened the window and thrust his head out as far as he could, his shoulders leaning against the window's frame. He arched and twisted his neck, looking as best as he was able toward the outside front of the bus, and then pulling it back in and looking up to the front of the bus where the woman was standing at the top of the steps. Elena followed Henri's lead and did the same on the empty seat in front of Henri. They both followed the woman's movement as she stepped down the stairs to the bus door and then quickly popped their heads out the window as she appeared to leave the bus. As they strained their necks they could see the large woman take a step off the bus and move to the outside. She seemed to start to turn her head as if to look around when suddenly she vanished. Henri's eyes opened wide and he could hear Elena suck in her breath. Their eyes were transfixed on the spot where the woman had been standing. Elena clutched Henri's arm which had been on the back of her seat. Henri looked at her and saw that the color had drained from her face. Elena's mouth moved and Henri knew what she was saying even though there were no words.

"Mama." Then she fainted and slumped onto Henri's side where he quickly caught her.

CHAPTER 10

His Name Is Will

No one who had witnessed the large woman's remarkable departure from the bus could speak. The weight of their paralyzing fear could be felt throughout the bus. One person who had no clue what happened was a man who had just stepped into the bathroom before the woman had left. To those who knew him he was called Mr. Hustle.

He was not, of course, born into this world as Mr. Hustle. His name was Will, but there were very few times when he was called Will. When he was a child, he was small and slightly pigeon-toed. He was nicknamed Peanut. It was cute then and he enjoyed the attention it gave him, but as he grew older, though not very much taller, the cuteness of it all dissipated and he found himself on the short end of what made up a memorably depressing childhood. He endured the humiliation of being picked last for a team, hearing other students snicker when he walked by, the label "Trippy Willy," and standing awkwardly and alone at school dances. The experiences made him tough and nearly bitter. He came up with a simple philosophy. He would work harder than anyone, rely on no one, and never let anyone tell him he couldn't do something. He lifted weights and learned to box so that if anyone did want to take advantage of his small stature with his weakened gait and challenge him physically, he would be more than able to make them think twice about trying it again.

He worked day jobs during high school to help save up for college. He had an average intelligence but like everything else he took on, he studied harder than most. He became so confident that he felt there was no need to believe in anything or anyone else. After college he landed a job at the ground floor of a company that manufactured parts for airplanes. His hard work and willingness to do any job earned him the title of Mr. Hustle, a title that stuck when the president of the company noticed him one day running about the warehouse checking inventory and inquired about the name. The president liked the nickname and when the president of a well-known international company wants to call you Mr. Hustle, God help that person who calls him anything different. Mr. Hustle worked his way up the ladder and in time became a regional supervisor over airplane manufacturing plants. His goal was to one day become the chief supervisor and enjoy the luxury of flying around the world inspecting not only the plants but the other regional inspectors. Until then, his travel was limited to cars, trains, and buses depending on which one was the most beneficial to the company. He did not like buses and as stepped out of the bathroom he did not like what he was hearing.

"She's gone," he heard a passenger say.

"What do you mean?" said another.

"We're stuck here. We can't leave."

"What's wrong?"

"Where did she go? Did something happen?"

"I'll never get off this bus if that's what's going to happen."

Meanwhile the bus driver sat immobile. He could not seem to turn away from viewing the desert floor just outside the door.

The stranger, who had been in the front seat, stood up and faced the remaining passengers.

"She disappeared. Three tried it last night and they have not returned. The bus driver tried to stop her. But it seems once you leave this bus, you leave it for good."

Henri could feel the hair stand up on the back of his neck. He had helped Elena back to her seat and she was still very pale.

A voice spoke up from the back of the bus. It was Mr. Hustle.

"I don't know what's going on but I'm going outside. I'll try to help fix the tire but if nobody is going to help then I'll just hitch hike the rest of the way. But I'm not staying put. I've got a job to do. This is nonsense and nobody tells me what I can and cannot do."

He walked purposefully to the front of the bus, the narrow isle making his slight pigeon-toed walk more obvious. All eyes followed him. No one seemed eager to stop him. There was an almost selfish feeling on the part of the other passengers that what happened was just too bizarre to believe and it would help if they could see it again just to be certain of this new reality. If the businessman wanted to go out no one was going to stop him.

Mr. Hustle stood by the door of the bus. His resolved seemed to weaken for a moment. There was an unearthly feel to the moment that he did not understand. He turned his head back toward the passengers. Silence engulfed the bus as they stared back at him as if he were a lab rat in an experiment. He looked down at the stranger sitting next to the bus driver. The expressionless look on his face was unnerving. The bus driver was looking down, unable to meet anyone's questions or gaze. Without as much confidence as he had when he started his walk down the aisle, Mr. Hustle hesitantly started to put one of his two feet outside the door and paused, as if to check if his foot would disappear. His foot hung in the air patiently waiting for his decision. By now, everyone except Henri and Elena had moved to the front by the window as close as they could.

The businessman pulled his foot back and it looked like he was going to retreat back into the bus, but to everyone's surprise, he stepped quickly off the bus and onto the desert ground. Just like the woman before him, he was gone as quick as a passing thought. There were audible gasps and shouts. One woman fainted. Another passenger kept himself from getting sick just long enough to make it into the bathroom. The stranger stood and stepped into the aisle and faced the remaining passengers.

"Anyone else?"

Just outside the bus, the sun beat down on Mr. Hustle. He stood still on the hot dirt floor feeling relief though he was not sure from what. Apparently whatever everyone was talking about had amounted to a lot of what he was feeling just then "a bunch of hot air." Fools, he thought to himself. He lifted both hands in the air, gave a shouting laugh, and jubilantly bellowed out, "nobody tells me what I can't do." Then he turned around. The bus was gone.

If he could see the passengers on the bus, he would see that the expression on his face mirrored the faces of those who had been watching him. Absolute incredulity. He spun around wildly, one direction after another, trying to see if the bus was anywhere, but all he saw was the empty, lonely desert.

"What…what?" was all he could cry out. He walked over to the large rock in front of the gas station and sat down. He tried to fight off an overwhelming sense of panic while sweat soaked through his shirt. The grinding heat from the sun made it impossible for him to think clearly. All of his life, the good and the bad, made some kind of sense to him but not this.

Eventually, he pulled himself together to explore around the gas station and see if there was a phone he could use to call for help. It did not take him long. On the front door was a sign posted which read "Out of business. No gas. No service. No phone. No bathroom." The sun was getting more and more unbearable and Will decided to pick up a rock and throw it at the window, thinking that if he could just get inside the shade might help him think. Just as he was about to let the rock fly he heard a car horn.

On the newer highway in the distance he could see a car pulled over and a hand waving out of the window, beckoning him to come. He dropped the rock and started to run as fast as he could with his pigeon-toes doing their best to keep him from falling. He knew he looked foolish but he did not care. The sun was melting him to a sloppy puddle and reality was slipping away. A lifeline had been thrown out to him from a place of sanity that had reason, not to mention air-conditioning. If he could just rest in a cool car and drive away maybe he could pretend that none of this had ever actually happened.

The car felt miles away while he flailed his legs, breathing heavily. By the time he reached the car he was nearly delirious with excitement, fatigue, and relief at seeing another human being. Exhausted from the agonizing run to the car he bent over and took deep breaths, trying not to pass out from the heat and fatigue. He did not hear the car doors open nor see the three men who stepped out, one of which carried a stick he concealed behind his back.

His boxing experience allowed him to get in a few good hits so that at least two of the men would regret taking him on, but three against one were odds that were just too great. While two of the men stood cursing him for their broken noses and black eyes, the other one took his wallet and gave him a couple of extra kicks while he was curled up on the pavement.

Will laid on the ground sucking in air and holding his ribs as the car sped off. For the moment, the only positive thing that happened was that the pain overshadowed the previous events and the scorching heat. Soon though, the pain, the heat, and the events melded into one hellish sense of desolation. Will drifted in and out of consciousness, images of the three men meshing together with night-marish childhood memories. His eyes and lips swelled. His lungs took in deep draughts of scorching heat. He would have tried to get up and leave if only he could move. The hours passed. Will tried to pray but he could not seem to put any words together. He knew there was a word for help but he could not remember what it was.

> *"They shall hunger no more, neither thirst any more, neither shall the sun light on them, nor any heat. For the Lamb which is in the midst of the throne shall feed them, and shall lead them unto living foundations of waters and God shall wipe away all tears from their eyes."*

Will opened his swollen eyes the best he could. He saw the faint outline of a figure. He could not tell if it was human or angelic. The voice was lovely and filled with light, laughter, and joy. With one hand it gently lifted his head and with the other brought a clear cup of water to his barely parted lips and gave him a sip.

"Be of good courage," said the voice. "The Master will take care of you." Its hand gently brushed his hair and Will felt a cool breeze just as he passed out.

Will slept. A bus drove by and pulled over. It was a small bus and on the side of the bus was written the words, "Blind Sisters for Jesus." A large man got out of the bus and picked Will up and carried him into the bus. He was taken to a home, which was not really a house, but an old hotel which had been converted into apartments. Next to that was another series of buildings used as an orphanage which was kitty-corner to a school, which stood across from a chapel, all of which wrapped itself in a half circle around a large flower garden. There were eight women on the bus who were all blind, and all sisters, and all for Jesus. They travelled wherever they were welcomed, singing and testifying of the Savior's desire to open the listeners' eyes. They were very eager to be Good Samaritans when the driver pulled the bus over and informed them that a man was lying on the road, bleeding and apparently unconscious.

Will recovered in one of the spare rooms. His eyesight never quite returned, leaving him for the rest of his days seeing everything in a dull blur. The beating brought on by the three young men left him deaf in one ear and with a very selective and unpredictable amnesia, such as his name, where he came from, and how he ended up on the desert floor in the middle of nowhere.

In time he fell in love with the place, their Savior, and one of the blind sisters whose name was Irene. Since he could not remember his name, he was content to let others try. None could come up with a name they all agreed on so that for some time he was just called Friend. Eventually they all agreed to just keep calling him Friend because it seemed to fit, except for the blind sister he later married, who called him something special that no one else knew. Friend started working a vegetable garden on the back side of the buildings, wearing a large sun hat, singing songs, and taking great joy kneeling in the dirt producing vegetables. The garden was blessed and grew and eventually a small vegetable stand was put up and customers starting coming and buying, and then more customers until it gained quite a reputation in the area. Friend never remembered the bus but he never forgot the visitor who gave him water.

CHAPTER 11

The Serpent, Who Is the Creature, Who Is the Beast

When Elena's mother first saw the bus it struck her as odd that she was looking at the back of the bus instead of the front. Kay distinctly remembered that when she first left the bus she had walked away from the front of the bus. How was it possible that upon finding the bus she should come across it from behind? But then again, everything about the night was odd. Could it be another bus further down the road? In the dull light that was around her she estimated that the bus was about a hundred yards away. In her eagerness to get back to Elena she decided to run toward the bus, however as soon as she had the thought to run she found that she was already there, standing next to a large flat rock. She slumped down on the rock.

"What in the world…!" she exclaimed. She turned and looked back to where she had just been but the pale light that had surrounded her before was gone and all that was visible was a thick black night with no shades of differentiation. It was as if a painter had painted black paint over the canvas of the sky, blotting out anything and everything that had illuminated the night. Within the confines of the buses perimeter a muted light continued so that she could see approximately twenty feet in any direction from the bus. The bus had become sort of an epicenter from which it was clear nothing could be achieved outside its parameters. She was at the back passenger side of the bus. The back tire was flat, so that either there were two buses on the same night with back rear flat tires or she had somehow managed to find the bus from the opposite direction from which she had left. At this point she could not tell which one was more unlikely. She felt as if she were floating with no sense or control of time, space, or movement. There were no rules about existence or physical matter, or if there were rules, they were beyond not only her understanding but also her ability to control them.

Kay anxiously looked into the windows of the bus and saw Elena. It did not occur to her until later that this was something she normally would not be able to do since the bus windows were too high up for someone to peer in. Apparently she was able to move or be where she wanted, but all she was thinking about was Elena.

She could see Elena sleeping on the lap of a boy about her age. Most of the passengers appeared asleep or at least attempting to sleep. Elena's mother pounded her fist on the window in an effort to get someone's attention but no would wake up and look her way. Kay then moved to the bus door and tried to push it open. She could feel her hands on the door but she could not sense any movement coming from the door. She tried banging on the door, producing the same useless results. The bus driver was asleep, his head slumped on the steering wheel. There was a young man with dark hair sitting upright in the front seat with his head turned toward her. It looked like he might be staring at her but she could not be sure. Pounding on the window and door did seem to make any difference. Kay went back to the rock and sat down, trying to think. For the first time since she left the bus she felt tired. She laid down on the rock on her back. After a few minutes, she went back to the window where she could see Elena. She pounded on the window again.

"Elena," she screamed as loud as she could.

"Yes, Mama," a voice quietly answered from behind her. It was Elena. She was sitting on the large rock, her feet dangling.

Elena's mother turned toward Elena.

"Elena?" The mother turned back toward the bus. Elena was still sleeping on the boy's lap.

The mother walked cautiously toward Elena and sat down on the rock.

"I don't understand." She looked back toward the bus. "How, Elena...?" Her voice trailed off.

"How what, Mama?"

The mother kept looking at Elena and then back at the bus.

"But you are with that boy."

"Oh, Henri. He's been so nice, Mama."

"But you are here and you are there. How is that possible?"

"I am here with you Mama," Elena answered plainly.

The mother moved toward the bus and called back to Elena.

"Come see," said the mother. "You are here, Elena."

Elena did not move. She patted the surface of the rock next to her, indicating that her mother was to sit with her. "I am here with you, Mama."

Slowly the mother moved back to Elena and sat down next to her. Elena slid her arm through her mothers and leaned her head on her shoulder.

"Are we going to be okay, Mama?"

Elena's mother stood and starting pacing back and forth.

"I don't understand," said the mother. "How can this all be? I was okay at first about how strange things felt, but this is different." She ran her fingers through her hair. "Oh, I wish I had a cigarette." She continued to pace back and forth and then suddenly stopped.

"Oh my, Elena, you can talk!"

Elena sat happily on the rock, her legs swinging.

"I know, Mama. Isn't it wonderful? Let's talk."

Elena's mother slumped down on the rock next to Elena and stared dumbly straight ahead. Elena grabbed her hand.

"Mama, why haven't you ever told me about my father?"

The question jarred Elena's mother and she turned to Elena. Her throat suddenly felt very dry.

"I, um...ah." She looked at Elena's face, filled with innocence. If she had been asked this question before she got off the bus she would have easily ignored it or changed the subject. She had only cared about her hurt. She realized now how hurt Elena must be to not have a father but she did not know how to answer her.

"He was a bad man, wasn't he, Mama?"

Elena was letting her off the hook. She was sparing her from telling the details by asking her a simple yes or no question. Her mother felt ashamed. Elena deserved so much better than this. The mother had cared only about herself and Elena had cared only about her mother.

"Yes, Elena, he was. Very bad."

Elena leaned her head on her mother's shoulder.

"You're not bad, mother. Just broken. Like me."

Tears rolled down the mother's face.

"I'm sorry, Elena. I'm sorry," she sobbed.

Kay woke up on the stone. She had fallen asleep. She sat up and wiped the tears from her face. What happened had felt so real but she decided it must have been a dream. She sat on the rock thinking about the dream, or vision, or whatever in the world was happening to her. Eventually she gave up trying to figure things out and took in what little surroundings were visible to her. The bus had managed to break down right in front of what appeared to be an abandoned gas station which added a mocking element to whatever it was that was being played out. There was a pay phone out front but the cord had been pulled off the side of the phone. She noticed the flat tire of the bus. She went over and took a closer examination but it was too dark to make anything out and even if she could see, she reasoned there was little she could do. She thought of sitting and the moment she did she found herself on the rock. The ability to be at a place without actually moving there was surprisingly annoying. Was she a ghost or some kind of phantom? She wondered that if she thought of her old apartment she would suddenly be there. She tried it without success. Apparently it only worked in this strange bubble around the bus.

She thought about the young boy that Elena was sitting with. If the dream she just experienced was more than a dream, then his name was Henri and he was somehow helping Elena. She vaguely remembered seeing a boy and man, who she assumed must be his father, sitting somewhere behind them on the bus. The mother envied the idea that the boy was comforting Elena. She felt a strong desire to be that comforter but she was grateful that at least someone was helping at the moment. She had no idea how long she had been away from the bus. Elena must have worried. She might even have tried to come out and find her.

It pained her that she could not remember ever trying to comfort her daughter. Ever since she had first seen her in the hospital with those eyes looking back at her all she secretly wanted was to be free from her. She could have given her up for adoption and had often considered it. She had even been encouraged by some to do so, but she had felt down inside that her husband's actions and those of the guard were somehow her fault and keeping Elena was a way to punish herself. However, as time wore on and Elena grew, the self-imposed verdict evolved into a self-imposed solitary that caused her to withdraw deeper and deeper into nothingness as a way to deal with the day to day reminder of her torturous world. To keep from looking at Elena with disgust, the mother clothed herself in a sort of dull deadness, putting on a mask not of false happiness, but of a deafening passivity. She knew this was a selfish act of self-preservation and deep down inside there was a large knot of guilt that she did her best to ignore.

She sat on the rock and meditated about this as if she were on the sofa of a psychiatrist, with full liberty, trying to explain how she felt. Then, for the first time, she saw all of what had transpired from a different angle. She had been horribly hurt and she fully hated how everything had turned out, but while better people than she might have managed, she saw that she might have done much worse with the results. She could have easily discarded Elena. For some reason she realized that she could not give Elena up and she saw this as an act of goodness, perhaps the first in her life. It might even be called a form of mercy. She admitted to herself that it was not something that was worth singing about from the highest mountain but it was a start for her. She still couldn't imagine showing mercy toward anyone else, including herself, but she began to feel that Elena not only deserved mercy but deserved whatever help she could give her.

"I will wait and see what I can do for her," the mother said firmly.

Hours passed, though they were not noticed, and the mother sat patiently on the rock. For every minute that passed the resolve to wait and watch grew within her. She might wait forever. Perhaps this was death and this was how she would spend eternity. She laughed out loud at the thought. There was a great joy in the thought that a small expenditure of goodness led to a greater capacity for more until the full measure of all that was good came to fruition only to find that there was infinite room for more. She swung her legs back and forth like a schoolgirl. Then she saw the snake.

At first it was difficult to tell if it was a small snake or a large worm. It was white with small black dots for eyes and if not for the fact that it slithered like a snake she would have mistaken it for a large worm. She was surprised because she did not know that a snake could be so short and thick, but in spite of the dark it was unmistakable. It was moving toward the front of the bus and even with the black night she could see it as clearly as she would up close on a sunny day. The snake did not seem to notice her as it made its way toward the door of the bus. She, like many, had a horrid fear of snakes. Kay moved quickly around the back side of the rock and crouched down and held her breath, watching as it approached the door of the bus. Then it did something entire out of the realm of a snake's ability. It stood up on its tail.

Even as it stood erect on the tip of its tail it was still a few inches short of the base of the door. She watched in horror as it balanced its body perfectly still and then almost gasped as it stretched its frame high enough to reach the door. There was a small opening at the base of the bus just high enough for the snake to rest its head. The sight was so unnatural that it did not occur to her at first what the snake was doing.

The snake somehow with one quick motion pulled its body up and slid through the small hole at the base of the door. The swiftness of the movement startled the mother. Kay could feel the hairs on her neck and arms stand up. There was something evil and diabolical about what had happened. She found herself at the window peering in.

There was no notice of the snake from any of the passengers. They gave the impression of being in a deep sleep except for the dark haired stranger in the front seat who appeared to be passively looking down at the floor of the bus. She followed the movement of the strangers head assuming that he was following the movement of the snake. A premonition of dread came over her that the snake might harm Elena. She was transfixed with a ghastly terror as she tried to follow the movement of the snake. Then, a few rows past the stranger, she saw the snake begin to grow taller; it's scaly skin stretching as it grew. Kay gasped and instinctively put her hand over her mouth. Slowly, right before her, the snake began to take on the form of a human. Oily arms started to sprout from the side of the creature with the scales falling to the side. At the end of the arms hands formed, followed by stocky wrinkly fingers. She noticed that there were no nails on the fingers. While this was happening the base of the torso split and two legs separated. The part of the creature that seemed to change the least was its head. Small ears sprouted and the front of the snakes face formed a more distinct nose. The eyes and mouth however continued to look like that of a snake. At one point, she even saw its tongue dart out, still thin and forked. As the creature was transmuting, portions of its skin were morphing into a cloth like substance resembling pale tan overalls over a shirt of similar color but with a slight variation in shading. By the time it reached Elena it had just finished its transformation and stopped. In the dark it looked enough like a man. An ugly and terrifying man, thought the mother, but a man nevertheless. The mother pounded as hard as she could on the windows, screaming for Elena to wake, for someone to help her, but just as before, no one noticed. The creature started to reach down toward Elena but then it slowly turned its head toward the stranger in the front and stopped. Then, without expression the creature walked calmly and mechanically toward the back of the bus and sat next to the window, staring straight ahead, eyes dull but never blinking.

Elena's mother, her fear and horror giving way to pure hatred of the creature glared at the creature-turned-man but it never looked back nor acknowledged that she was even there. The mother felt completely helpless and alone. Whatever this was it had to be stopped. She rested her forehead on the window and closed her eyes. The faint whisper of a prayer formed in her spirit. There were no words spoken, just a pleading thought that the God she did not know would help the daughter she had never loved. Kay opened her eyes and found herself face to face with the stranger. She was still on the outside of the bus but her face was close to the window. The stranger was inches away on the inside looking at her and this time the mother could see in the strangers face that he saw her. Her eyes lit up and she smiled broadly. She had forgotten how wonderful it was to be acknowledged, to have contact with another person. Kay gave a pleading gesture and motioned toward the monster in the back. The stranger gave a slight smile and in that smile the mother perceived in a moment that the creature and the stranger had somehow known each other for a very long time and that they were enemies. The creature was evil and the stranger was not. Without a word being said she understood that the creature was there for a purpose and that purpose had something to do with Elena. She also understood that the stranger was in the bus for a purpose and that purpose was Elena's welfare. Everything that had happened since she first stepped off the bus was to prepare her for her purpose, though she did not know what it was. Kay was outside the bus for a reason. She would continue to wait. Knowing that she had an ally of sorts inside gave her courage for whatever she would have to do when the time came. The mother went back to the rock and sat.

CHAPTER 12

The Thief

Thorton had spent most of his childhood planning mischief, getting into mischief, and trying to escape mischief. At least that was the word used about him when he was a child. However, in his later teen years mischief turned into lawlessness. Planning jobs, getting arrested, and attempting escapes became his way of life. Abandoned by his mother on the doorstep of an orphanage, he never knew what a parent was, only what a "guardian" was. Later in life he thought it was amusing that the word guardian and guard were so similar. Maybe amusing was not the right word. Fitting, but seldom amusing.

Until he was fourteen he had bounced back and forth between orphanages and foster homes. He liked the consistency of the orphanage because of the low expectations. There was a reliability in knowing he would be fed and clothed but not cared for. The foster homes were a mixed bag. Some made the orphanages seem almost hospitable. Others were unbearably kind, and in a strange way, this was harder for him to accept. It was easier for him to have no expectations, and have to fight and scratch for what he wanted. He could never understand why strangers wanted to help him. Thorton always felt there was a hidden motive somewhere and if he gave in to their advances of human compassion he eventually would disappoint or be disappointed ending up more broken than he already was. He decided at an early age that he would live for himself and fight anyone who tried to stop him.

At fourteen, Thorton had upset another foster family. They had suspected him of stealing some money from the small savings their daughter had kept hidden in a closet. They were right in suspecting him, even though Thorton by then had become quite the good liar and story teller. They were a kind family but they realized that with Thorton they were in over their heads and asked that he be returned to the orphanage. Thorton decided that he had had enough and left in the night, taking not only the money from the daughter but also the mother's jewelry box. He would spend the remaining teen years on the road, thieving and living on the streets out of the eyes of those who would rule over him.

Thorton was a good thief, good in the sense that he was very capable. He acquired mentors in the field and learned how to pick-pocket, shoplift, break into a building undetected and leave without a trace. After he had learned all that he could from someone, he would leave them suddenly and move on to another city. He learned how to act in order to get what he needed. He could turn on the charm when he wanted even though he despised being liked and trusted. To him, being personable was a tool, no different than a pair of wire cutters, and conning people was a necessary evil. He did not hate them and he refused violence as an option for getting what he wanted or needed. He knew there were good people and he knew there were bad people. Thorton assumed he was bad, not because of what he did, but because he rejected kindness. It was easier to keep his distance from others. Sooner or later he knew he would let them down, so it was best to get it over quickly and keep the pain he was certain to inflict on them to a minimum. It was who he was.

By the time Thorton was twenty-four he had done a few stints in jail for theft. He hated prison, not for the obvious reasons, but because it reminded him so much of the orphanage life he had fled. It wasn't just the confinement and the order enforced by the guards that bothered him. It was the close proximity of others that drove him nearly insane. As a result, just like when he was a young teen flee-ing the orphanage, he always found a way to escape. Once freed, he would lie low, get some new identification papers, move to another city, and begin again.

During his last time in prison, Thorton had been walking past the kitchen and noticed a lifer passing a shiv to a thief. This particular thief, whose name was Hudson, Hud for short, had tried to make friends with Thorton as a fellow thief but Thorton had repeatedly steered clear of Hud. Thorton passed the kitchen and went to his cell. Two days later, the leader of one of the gangs in the prison had been stabbed to death and it was suspected that Hud had been responsible. Thorton had never told anyone what he had seen in the kitchen, but from that moment on, Hud determined that Thorton had squealed and that he would get even someday. Thorton had been planning an escape through the ventilation ducks but was still in the planning stages. He knew that he might have to risk it even if he felt unprepared. While Hud was doing some preparation of his own for revenge, Thorton took his chance and escaped.

Two years later, Thorton, having escaped from prison, fled to another city and was back to his solitary lifestyle of thieving. One day, unbeknownst to him, he was spotted by Hud on a busy street. Hud had been found innocent of the murder of the prisoner due to insufficient evidence. He had finished his sentence and been set free. He had promised himself that if he ever found Thorton he would make him pay for snitching on him. He could not believe his luck the day he spotted Thorton while Hud was climbing into a taxi. Initially, Hud's idea was to simply follow Thorton into a secluded place and kill him, but after a while he decided it might be more fitting to try and frame him for something. For months he followed Thorton, discovering where he lived, his daily routine, and watching him set up and pull jobs. Hud waited for just the right opportunity. One day it came. He could see that Thorton had found a rich man outside the city who had poor security on his house. It would be an easy score for Thorton once the mark had left the house. One day, while Thorton was out, Hud snuck into Thorton's apartment and found a knife that he felt Thorton would not notice missing for some time.

He watched Thorton, thief to thief, and knew from his pattern which night Thorton would attempt to break in. Hud sat still that night waiting in the shadows and watched the rich man leave. Then he saw Thorton silently enter the house and after some time, leave with his haul. Hud continued to wait until the rich man came back. That's when he made his move. He quietly broke into the rich man's house, killed him with Thorton's knife and left. Two days later Hud made an anonymous call to the police stating that he had read about the murder of the rich man and had seen a man at a particular apartment.

Thorton was arrested. A quick raid on Thorton's apartment produced the rich man's valuables. Thorton was taken to a small local jail. The prints on the knife matched his prints but the police were having difficulty matching his prints with the ID that Thorton had on him. They assumed that the ID had been forged but it would take some time to figure out who Thorton really was and Thorton was not going to volunteer any information. But he knew it would just be a matter of time before the connection was made. In the meantime, the one advantage Thorton had was that they thought he was a murderer who stole and not an experienced thief who had been accused of murder. If they had known Thorton's history of escaping prisons, they would have been much more careful. Security was somewhat lax due to staffing and Thorton could pick just about any lock, and the lock here was no exception. Late at night with the sole desk guard sleeping with a magazine in his lap, Thorton managed to escape. He made his way down a side street and found a car he could hot wire. Thorton drove for a few miles thinking about how long before he could ditch his current car for another, when he passed a bus station. Thorton drove about a hundred yards pass the bus station and found a convenient place to hide the car so that it would not be seen without some effort. He walked back to the bus station and found that a bus was just leaving. Thorton managed to pick the pocket of someone heading into the men's room as he was leaving. He quickly pocketed the cash, trashed the wallet, and bought a ticket. He boarded the bus just before it departed. There was an empty seat toward the back behind an elderly couple. Thorton sat down low as the bus pulled out. Hours later the bus blew a tire and he found himself sitting in the dead of night with a bus full of angry passengers.

There was nothing he could do. The night was so dark that he had no idea which way to go. The only thing he could do was follow the road but that would increase his chance of the police seeing him. To go off into the desert without any sense of direction or terrain would be just as risky. He would just have to wait until morning. Until then he would have to lie low and hope for the best. Thorton sat quietly in his seat while the other passengers vented their frustration. The elderly woman in front of him turned around and smiled.

"You don't seem too bothered by all this fuss," she said calmly to Thorton.

Thorton smiled awkwardly. "Well, what are you gonna do? These things happen."

"What things?" she asked quizzically, with a slight smile on her face. Thorton felt as if she were playing a game of cat and mouse. He knew he was nervous and tried his best to stay calm.

"Flat tires, I suppose."

"Oh, yes..." replied the lady, briefly pausing. "Flat tires. They do happen."

Thorton couldn't tell if he was just being paranoid or not, but it sounded as if she put the emphasis on the word "they."

"My name's Gladys. What is yours, young man, if you don't mind me asking?"

"Uh, Bill. Bill Smith. Nice to meet you."

"Nice to meet you too, Mr. Smith. I can see that I probably have pestered you enough. I'll let you get your rest. Thank you."

Thorton was glad to end the conversation but was surprised that she thanked him.

"Thank you for what?" asked Thorton.

"Why, for your company and the pleasure of your time."

Thorton felt and look dumbfounded. He wasn't used to a conversation of this nature.

"Uh, you too," was all he could think of answering.

Gladys turned around. She leaned her head on her husband's shoulder. Thorton decided it was best to pretend to be sleeping so that no one else would try and approach him. He closed his eyes and worried about the night. Eventually the night took over and he slept soundly.

Thorton awoke later than he had planned. He had wanted to get out at first light and try to get a good jump on fleeing but he had slept so soundly that he felt as if he had been drugged. He woke just in time to see the soldier step off the bus but was not aware of what the others had seen. By the time the loud, large woman stepped off, Thorton was standing with his head thrust out the window straining to see a woman step onto the ground and suddenly vanish.

"Imagine that," said the elderly woman to her husband.

Thorton slumped back into his seat. There had to be some mistake, he thought. He leaned his head back out the window and looked around. All that could be seen was what looked like an old abandoned gas station. He turned his head and looked out the other window. He would see a car occasionally pass by but there was no sign of the two who had left. He decided to walk toward the front of the bus and look down the road. He stopped just behind the bus driver and put one hand on the pole opposite the driver's seat. He stretched his head forward and scanned the empty horizon.

"Wonder where they went," said a man in the front row. Thorton looked down at him. The man was young with dark black hair and seemed completely relaxed. If the man had a newspaper, Thorton could picture him with his feet up reading the paper without a care in the world. He didn't seem to wonder at all where they went. Thorton looked at the bus driver. His face was pale as he stared straight ahead, his hands clutching the wheel so tightly his knuckles were white. Thorton turned around and went back to his seat.

He must have missed something, he thought. This is ridiculous. People don't disappear. Thorton was about to get up again and head to the front when someone came out of the bathroom door behind him. It was a man in a suit, not cheap and not expensive. Because of the commotion that was going on the man demanded to know what was happening. The man decided that he was going to leave. Thorton put his head out of the window and watched the man disappear.

Thorton, like most of the other passengers, found himself now trying to not only comprehend what was happening but what he was going to do about it. His natural instinct was to run. That's what he had always done when the heat was on. Now, more than ever, he needed to be somewhere else. He was too close to the jail and by now the cops would be looking for him. If a cruiser happened to pass the bus it would most likely stop. They would probably do more than just try to help fix the tire, they would be looking for any one matching the description of the escaped murderer. Perhaps there was a perfectly acceptable reason for people disappearing when they stepped off the bus that no one had considered. But Thorton felt frozen in fear. He couldn't move, so for a few hours he watched and waited.

Every now and then a passenger would walk to the front of the bus and stand on the lowest step. A horrible silence would come over the bus. Most attempts would start out with the potential candidate taking a step out into the unknown and let their foot hoover before bringing it back in and slinking back to their seat. One young man pulled his wallet out of his pants pocket and tossed it to the ground to see if it would disappear. It did not disappear and instinctively the man stepped down to pick it up and was gone, proving not only that material items outside the bus did not disappear but also the old axiom that a fool and his money are soon parted.

Another passenger, perhaps in pursuit of scientific inquiry, answered the question whether the effect would take place if one simply reached out and touched the ground with one finger. Depending on one's point of view, probably not his, the experiment was a success. Thorton watched as a few left out of a sense of inevitability, with a let's get this over mindset while some others left out of a sense of adventure. One thoughtful, athletic person pondered the possibility that the powers that be were confined to the immediate proximity at the base of the step and attempted to leap as far as he could only to find that there was either no proximity or that he overestimated his leaping abilities.

It began to dawn on Thorton that he did not have an option. Eventually he would either step out into the unknown or be picked up by a passing cop and spend the rest of his life in jail. He decided that the fear of the unknown was better than the bleakness of the known. He stood and stretched his legs.

"I think you're making the right decision," said the old woman who turned around when he stood.

"How do you know I made a decision?" asked Thorton.

"I have been praying for you all night. I think its best that you leave."

"Okay…thanks, I guess," said Thorton. "But I don't really believe in God."

"Well, of course not dear. No one does at first. That's why you're here."

Thorton did not know how to respond to that. He began to think that just getting away from this kooky woman was reason enough to leave. He walked toward the front of the bus and without hesitation stepped off.

For Thorton, stepping off the bus was like entering into a dream where you start in the middle of an action without any prelude to how it began. He found himself walking up a hill on a small path and immediately stopped. He was no longer in the same desert. The air was not as hot and there was more vegetation. He was on a dirt path. He looked at his clothes. He was wearing some type of cloth garment that extended from his neck to his feet. He had a cloth belt tied at the waist and had a full length open robe covering him. He peered down at his feet. His shoes and socks were gone, replaced by a pair of flat sandals. He turned around to see the bus.

The bus was barely visible. It appeared to be at the base of the hill that Thorton had apparently been climbing. Coming up the hill was a man, dressed like Thorton but carrying a staff. It was the husband of the elderly woman who had sat in front of him on the bus. When the old man reached Thorton he stopped and leaned on his staff taking in deep breaths.

"Pardon me," he said. "The walk winded me."

"Am I dreaming?" asked Thorton. "I mean, that's probably a stupid question to ask in a dream but this is so real and so unreal that I don't know what to make of it."

"No," answered the man. "I don't believe so. I'm not sure if we're dead either if that was your next question. But it is definitely unique. We're certainly not in the same place and time as we were, judging by this hill and our clothes."

Thorton scanned the horizon. "This is definitely a different place. I wonder if this is what happened to the others who left the bus. Maybe we should try to find them. By the way, why are you here? Why did you leave the bus?"

The man smiled. "When you left, I had this impulse to follow you. I've learned over time that usually means the Lord is leading me." The man shrugged his shoulders, knowing that what he was saying probably sounded foolish to the young man.

They stared at each other awkwardly for some time. Finally Thorton spoke up.

"Well, what do we do now? Do you think we should go back to the bus? Maybe we should warn the others."

"I have a feeling that just because we can see the bus doesn't mean that it is still there. You can try if you want, but I don't have the energy," answered the man. "By the way, my name is Holger."

"Thorton. Hey, you left your wife on the bus?"

"Yes, I know," answered Holger. "But Gladys has her own impulse right now and that is the care of the girl."

"The girl?"

"Yes, the mute. Gladys is protecting her."

"What? How and why?" asked Thorton a little irritated about the nature of the conversation.

"She believes the girl is important. 'How' is something I don't think you are ready to talk about yet."

Just then a loud roar was heard from the other side of the hill.

Thorton looked at Holger.

"We might as well find out what this is all about," said Holger. "I kind of like this staff." With that, he planted it a step ahead of him and continued up the hill.

They followed the narrow path for about fifteen minutes before reaching the top. Holger sat down. He had a cloth that rested over his shoulders. He pulled it up and over his head.

"I don't believe it," he said solemnly.

Thorton sat down next to Holger.

"What is it? Where are we? Do you know?"

Holger said the word, almost in a whisper.

"Jerusalem."

Thorton looked down at the city. It was bustling with people but there were no cars or buses or modern buildings. Instead, there were animals and carts.

"You mean, like the Bible Jerusalem?"

"Yes," answered Holger. "And more Bible than you know. It is not just Jerusalem from the Bible. It is Jerusalem during the time of Christ."

"How do you know?" asked Thorton.

Holger pointed toward the base of the hill near a building.

"Because I think that's Him."

Thorton looked to where Holger was pointing. He could see a crowd of men standing in a semi-circle around a man who was talking to them. Holger had gotten up and was heading quickly down the hill toward Jesus. Thorton stood and reluctantly followed him. There were about twenty men gathered around Jesus listening intently. No one seemed to notice Holger and Thorton as they joined them. Holger tried to get as close as he could while Thorton hung toward the back.

"And you shall be hated by all for my name's sake. But not one hair of your head will perish. In your patience possess your souls." There was a pause after this as Jesus seemed to look intently at each listener. As his eyes caught Thortons, Thorton could feel himself turn red and lowered his head. When he looked back up, Jesus was smiling at him. Then he made a slight motion with his hand and started walking away, his disciples following him. Holger and Thorton stood still as they walked away.

"Wait here. I'll be right back," said Holger as he went over to a man by a table.

Thorton wanted to ask Holger where he was going but he could not seem to get any words out. He stood dumbfounded. This was beyond religion, beyond understanding, beyond anything his simplistic philosophy of life had ever presented to him. He walked over to a large stone and sat down. What was happening?

Holger returned after talking to the man and Thorton stood up.

"What was that about?"

"Can you believe it?" said Holger excitedly. "Jesus Christ, the Messiah! We stood right here listening to him speak. I've read those words over and over through the years and now I have heard the spoken word from the Living Word."

"I don't understand. Look, I may not know too much about all this religious stuff, but didn't they speak a different language? How can we understand them and what does this all mean?" said Thorton.

"It's fascinating," replied Holger. "I spoke with a gentleman at the table and to my surprise he understood every word I said to him. I don't know how it's all happening but I will tell you what I have learned. We are at the time of the Passover."

"So," said Thorton, "what's the Passover?"

"It's a Jewish celebration of Israel's deliverance from Egypt during the time of Moses."

"I don't know any of this stuff. These names sound familiar but it all means nothing to me."

Holger put his hand on Thorton's shoulder.

"I know. Just because the details are more familiar to me does not mean that it's not equally fantastic. But we have come at a momentous time. We are at the crossroads of history."

"What do you mean?" asked Thorton.

"Tomorrow, Jesus will be betrayed by one of his disciples. The Jewish leaders have been looking for an opportunity to kill him. It will be a time of great sorrow. But after three days He will rise from the dead. He is paying for the sins of all mankind. We are at the end and we are at the beginning."

"Should we try to stop them?" Thorton said with concern in his voice.

"No, my friend. That we most certainly shouldn't do. He was sent by God for this very purpose. We are here for other reasons."

"I'd sure like to know what," said Thorton. Just as Holger was about to answer him, a voice cried out.

"Thief! There he is. That is the man." The voice crying out was pointing his finger at Thorton.

Before Thorton had a chance to consider running, a Roman soldier grabbed one of Thorton's arms with an iron grip.

"You may have eluded us once thief. It will not happen again."

"You got the wrong man," cried out Thorton. "I don't even live here. Help me Holger," pleaded Thorton. Holger started to step toward the soldier.

"One step closer old man and that head of yours will come off. Move back!" He pushed roughly past Holger, sending him to the ground. Holger could see Thorton's face turning around, calling out desperately as the soldier hurried off with him. Holger tried to follow but the soldiers pace was too fast and the crowd of people became more dense as he moved toward the center of the city.

Thorton was dragged through the streets of Jerusalem, shouting out his protests of innocence to no avail. He was either ignored by those who had seen the sight too often or shunned by those who felt disdain. A few spit on him as he was pulled through the streets, careful not to hit the soldiers as they did so. The Roman soldiers grip was unrelenting and did not relax until they had reached a building where another soldier opened a door and the one holding Thorton threw him on the floor. There were three other soldiers in the building. Thorton did a quick glance around to see if there were any possible ways of escape.

"Keep your eyes on this one, men. If he looks familiar it's because he's the one who managed to escape last week. He'll be on the cross tomorrow, so chain him to the wall and the gods of Rome help anyone who sleeps or lets him get away again. Are you hungry, thief?"

Thorton had been thinking about food ever since leaving the bus.

"Yes, I am."

"Too bad, thief." The soldiers laughed heartily. One of the soldiers sitting at a table walked over to Thorton and without a word lifted him easily with one arm and threw him toward an open door. Thorton fell through the doorway and onto the cold floor of the room. There were chains attached to the wall with shackles.

The guard stepped into the doorway, filling it with his broad shoulders. He pointed to a corner of the room.

"There," was all he said as he pointed to a corner in the room. In doing so, he made it clear to Thorton that Thorton could move on his own or be tossed like a rag doll. Thorton quickly scampered to the corner. The guard connected the shackles to Thortons hands and feet. The chains were long enough for Thorton to sit or lean against the wall but not stand up or lie down completely. There were no windows in the room and even with the afternoon sun coming through the main entrance, the room was dark. The only way out of the jail was through the door and past at least one guard who had been warned to never sleep. This simple setting seemed more daunting to Thorton than any modern prison from which he had escaped. A wave of exhaustion and depression came over him as he dropped his head onto his chest.

"So the ghost has returned." It was a voice from the other corner of the room. A man sat chained to the far wall. Thorton had not noticed him. The man sat on the side of the room that picked up some of the light through the doorway. While most of his body was in the shadows his face was exposed to the light. He had a scraggily beard and matted hair. On his face was a scar that ran from the outer corner of his eye down toward his chin. He had deep set eyes and a long hook nose. It was a very distinct face and completely surprised Thorton.

"Hud?" asked Thorton incredulously.

"What, Ghost?"

"Hud?" repeated Thorton. "Is that you?"

"What are you talking about Ghost? What's a hud?"

"Hud. Short for Hudson. It's a name. Are you Hud?"

"What kind of strange name is Hud?" answered the prisoner. "No, I am not Hud, Ghost. And even if it was, it doesn't matter anymore. We are thieves. That is our name, Ghost."

"Why do you keep calling me Ghost?" asked Thorton.

"Because, Ghost, you disappeared."

Thorton's eyes opened wide. "You know about the bus?"

"Bus…what, by Zeus, is a bus? You have the strangest words, Ghost."

"Why did you say I've disappeared?"

"You were in the rich man's house. The soldiers had you trapped in one of his rooms, gold coins in hand. Then you were gone. How did you do it? I heard you were good, but that vanishing act was what makes legends. If it makes you feel better, I stuck the old man a day later and took his money. I almost made it out too but I was caught hiding in the caves."

"What do you mean, stuck the old man?" asked Thorton.

The prisoner brought his hand to his throat and made a slicing motion, then laughed.

Thorton stared intently at the prisoner. While everything that had happened since he stepped off the bus made no sense, one thing suddenly because very clear to Thorton.

"You killed the rich man, Hud. You thought I ratted you out in prison when you gave that shank to that man in the kitchen. You set me up after I robbed that rich guy. You planted the knife and called the cops. It was you Hud who framed me for that murder."

Thorton put his hand to his forehead and rubbed his temples. "I can't believe I didn't see it before. It was you all along."

The prisoner looked at Thorton as if he were deranged.

"You must be filled with a demon, Ghost. Your words don't make sense. It doesn't matter anyway. Tomorrow we both die on the cross. And keep your mouth shut. The guards are angry enough at us already. We will pay for that tomorrow before they crucify us."

"What do you mean?" asked Thorton.

"We are sport," answered the prisoner. "They can do with us as they will. Have you never seen a crucifixion? The beating and scourging before can sometimes kill a man."

There was nothing more to be said. Thorton sat uncomfortably on the cold floor trying to reason why he was here and if there was any way he could get out of it. In the past his mind seemed to be at its sharpest when things were at their worst but now he felt as if every thought found its way to a dead end. He was in a maze with a sealed off entrance and no exit. A great depression and sense of dread flooded his soul. It was impossible to sleep. His stomach roared in hunger and he felt that he had not had anything to drink for days.

Just before dawn he finally fell asleep only to be kicked in the side by the guard.

"Up, thief," growled the guard as he unshackled Thorton. Another guard was doing the same to the other prisoner.

"I'm looking forward to this, thief. You got me in a lot of trouble by disappearing like that. I don't know how you did it, but you will pay today."

"But you have the wrong man," pleaded Thorton.

"First you fool me, and now you insult my intelligence. A stripe for every word. Please keep talking, thief."

Thorton held his tongue while the guard pulled him outside the jail and toward a back wall that held more chains. These were higher up the wall and were shorter in length than the ones in the cell. The wall was covered with blood stains. Thorton was put face first against the wall and secured. His robe and undergarment were ripped off and a second later came the first of many scorching pains across his back and around his side as the whip penetrated his flesh.

Thorton lost track of time and counts the whip had flailed his skin. It seemed it would never end, but at some point, he heard laughter and one of the guards came over and freed him. Thorton fell to the ground but was quickly picked up by one of the guards who held him upright. Thorton barely had his eyes open when he saw a fist coming fast at his head.

"That's for my trouble," grunted the guard as Thorton fell to the ground unconscious.

He was dragged over an open court and thrown on the ground.

"You better not have killed him Marcus," said one of the guards.

"He's not dead," answered Marcus. "I've hit enough men to know. Throw some water on his face and stand him up."

Thorton was stood up. His ear was ringing and his left eye was swelling up. One of the guards slapped his face.

"Wake up, thief. Time to work for your death."

Thorton was led by two guards to a wall. One of the guards left and the other continued to hold Thorton. Thorton put one hand on the wall to help hold himself up. Moments later a weight was placed on his shoulder and back sending bolts of pain down his legs and through his chest. Thorton screamed out.

"Nothing like carrying your own cross to wake up a man. I told you I didn't kill him," said Marcus. Marcus gave a loud laugh.

"Let's go, thief. Time for our morning walk. Now, I'm not carrying you. You walk or you get whipped. You understand?"

Thorton nodded.

Thorton marched along doing his best not to feel the slash of Marcus whip against his back. He had lost track of the lashes and he had lost track of time. He felt as if he would never stop walking. His legs shook as he stumbled through the dusty streets swaying back and forth, trying to keep his balance. His back burned like a raging fire and his head pounded. His left eye was now completely shut and he could only hear out of his right ear. People lined the streets as if it were a parade. Some spat on him like they were throwing confetti.

"This one has strong legs, Marcus," said one of the soldiers.

"Good," answered Marcus. "The longer he is up, the more he suffers. Where are the other two?"

"They are almost there."

"They we must pick up the pace. Faster, thief!" yelled Marcus as he put the whip to Thorton's back.

There was a good crowd watching as Thorton reached his destination. One of the guards took the cross off of his shoulders and Thorton fell to his knees. Before he had time to take in a deep breath he was pushed down to the ground and laid on his back on top of the cross. He was kicked hard by one of the guards as an incentive to hurry. As Thorton lay on the cross his back burned with fresh bursts of shooting pain and Thorton gasped. One of the guards slid Thorton down toward the bottom of the cross until Thorton felt a flat piece of wood against his feet. Two guards, one on each side, grabbed Thorton's arms and stretched them out. Thorton heard a loud bang and felt a fiery pain shoot through his feet and then through each hand.

His eyes opened wide in horror as he was lifted up and the cross secured. The weight of his body caused him to sink and he felt his feet cling to the piece of wood below them. As he did so a horrendous pain shot through him and he could barely breathe.

Thorton went mad with pain. He screamed out a yell that pierced to the depths of his being. He cursed. He cursed the pain. He cursed the God that made the earth. He cursed his father whom he never knew. He cursed his mother for abandoning him. He screamed and cursed and cursed and screamed. He was insane with pain and hatred and he did not care who heard or saw. He cursed the other thief who he saw was also screaming. He cursed the man in the middle who held on silently. He cursed him for his silence. He cursed the crowd for their noise. He cursed the soldiers who mocked him. He cursed until his throat was too raw to barely make a noise.

"I am innocent," he whimpered.

Thorton sensed the man in the middle had turned his head toward him as he spoke. Thorton looked at the man. The face was so beaten and bloodied that he would not have recognized him except for the eyes. They were the eyes of the man named Jesus who had beheld him the day before. While there was no fear or dread in them, Thorton could see that there was intense sorrow and pity. Like the day before, Thorton hung his head, this time not in embarrassment, but in shame. He wasn't innocent. He was a thief. What was worse was that he was a murderer also. Even though Hud had actually killed the rich man, he never would have died had Thorton not robbed him first. What did it matter how or when it had happened. Whether it was thousands of years ago or last week. He had spent his life selfishly, justifying it by the pain he felt at being abandoned. He had forsaken the help of others for fear of failing them and being abandoned again. When he looked back into the eyes of Jesus he could see the same smile in them as the other day. Somehow Jesus knew Thorton's pain. Thorton could see it in his eyes. Jesus looked at him as though he felt the same way even though Thorton knew that somehow this man could never be guilty of anything. Just then the other thief, the one who looked like Hud, starting railing at Jesus.

"If you are the Christ, save yourself and us."

"Don't you fear God? You're just as guilty. We deserve this, but this man has done no wrong," answered Thorton with all the strength his voice could muster. His legs buckled from weakness and as they collapsed pain shot through his body and he felt his breath shorten. Slowly he pushed himself back up, his raw back scrapping the wood. He tried to arch his back away from the wood. In doing so, he saw the writing above Jesus head on the cross. "The King of the Jews." Thorton moistened his lips the best he could and took a shallow breath.

"Lord, remember me when you come into your kingdom."

"Be certain, that today you shall be with me in paradise," said Jesus.

A great peace engulfed Thorton. All of the pain and the guilt washed away. He closed his eyes and said his first prayer of thanks. As he did so, he heard a gasp from the crowd and opened his eyes. Darkness suddenly started to descend all about them. He could hear some of the crowd cry out in fear. The soldiers barely visible below appeared to be shocked and doing their best to hold their composure. Thorton looked over at Jesus, his head hung low.

For the next few hours the darkness continued. Thorton continued to alternate between giving his legs a break from standing and trying to breathe. He knew a time would come when he could not hold out any longer and he would no longer be able to stand. The body's instinct for survival kept him from giving up but he knew it could only last so long.

The words of Jesus from the previous day came back to Thorton. "In your patience, possess you your souls." Thorton had never read the Bible and could not quote a single verse but he now understood its power. Every word seemed to have meaning and power. He decided he would patiently hold out as long as he could without complaining. At one point he looked into the crowd and thought he saw Holger but he could not be sure. One eye was swollen shut and the other was filled with blood.

Then suddenly Jesus cried out, "Father, into your hands, I commit my spirit." Thorton, whose head was down looked over at Jesus. Jesus head was also down and his body slumped down further, his arms extended from the pulling down of his body. It was clear he was dead. There was a great silence from the crowd. After a few minutes Thorton noticed one of the soldiers go to the other thief with a large pole and swing heavily against his knees. Thorton heard the thief gasp before sliding down. He tried to push up with his feet but his legs would not straighten, instead the bones separated, which caused the thief to scream out. After a few moments the thief made an effort to gasp for breath but none came and he passed out. The soldier walked over to Thorton. Thorton closed his eyes and whispered "today you shall be with me in paradise," as he heard a loud crunch and felt his legs buckle.

Holger was back on the bus. He didn't know how. He had been watching Thorton from a distance. The moment he saw the soldier break his legs Holger closed his eyes as a natural reaction against the horror of the moment, and when he opened them, he was back on the bus sitting next to Gladys. He looked around at the other passengers, expecting them to say something about his disappearance and reappearance but no one seemed either to know or care.

Gladys clasped his hand.

"I think it's time for us to leave."

"The girl? Will she be all right?" asked Holger.

"The stranger is here. There will be an attempt made but it is beyond us now."

While no one other than the stranger had seen the snake creature board the bus it was obvious to all that an extra passenger was sitting silently in the back seat. His skin was pale white, his head, face and arms were hairless, and he had unusually small eyes, which stared straight ahead emotionless and unexpressive. He was wearing a smudged white undershirt, a pair of grease stained overalls and had on no shoes or socks. No one had the nerve to ask the man anything, much less look at him directly. Everyone had moved a little closer to the front except Gladys, who had positioned herself nearer the little girl.

The bus driver sat silently in his seat, seldom getting up, engulfed in guilt. The weight of the circumstances seemed to force his head and shoulders down so low that he sometimes found himself leaning heavily on the steering wheel, unable or desirous to rouse himself to an upright position. There had been many fruitless recriminations the first day or two from some of the more outspoken passengers about this being entirely his fault. Many felt that they would be justified in tossing the bus driver out the door. In spite of the man next to him consistently defending him, the bus driver could not help but feel it was true. If he could resolve it somehow, he would in a second. No matter what the cost. No matter what.

Gladys and Holger approached the front of the bus. The bus driver had noticed that there was a calmness to them that intrigued him and also made him envious. He wanted to ask them about it but he couldn't seem to shake himself from the cloud of gloom and guilt that enveloped him.

"Excuse me," said the elderly man. "Could you please open the door? We would like to leave now."

The bus driver looked up. He felt like a child in school not understanding what was being said to him by the teacher.

"What do you mean?" he responded slowly.

The woman smiled and said warmly.

"I think it's time for us to leave."

"What do you mean, time for us?" asked the bus driver.

The older man answered.

"We are ready to go. I am not sure if we are dead already but Jesus is calling us home and we are ready to go. So if we are dead, then we would like to meet our Master and if this is not death, then we trust Him with what will happen next. He has not failed us all these years. He will not fail us now."

The bus driver felt an intense longing to have the peace he saw on their faces. They seemed almost childlike with no sense of fear and only a revelation of joy and excitement about what they had and what they were facing. He had never envied anyone so much in all of his life.

Suddenly the elderly woman grabbed the bus drivers arm and brought her face close to his. The bus driver smelled a faint odor of her lilac perfume. Her tender eyes pierced through him like a sword. The bus driver turned red. It felt like she could see right through him and that she knew everything about him. He was suddenly seized with a sense of fear and dread that she might turn to others on the bus and shout out what he had done. Instead she leaned over and whispered into his ear.

"Peace I leave with you, my peace I give unto you: not as the world giveth, give I unto you. Let not your heart be troubled, neither let it be afraid."

The bus driver didn't see what happened next. He didn't see the elderly couple wave good-bye to the remaining passengers. He didn't see them confidently step off the bus steps. He didn't see them vanish because his face was buried in his hands as he quietly wept.

CHAPTER 13

The Call of Henri

Throughout the days and nights, Henri spent most of his time at Elena's side. For the remaining adult passengers on the bus an unimaginable terror gripped them like a vice. With the exception of the two strangers at either end of the bus and perhaps Henri's uncle who kept his sanity by focusing on Henri's well-being, everyone was frozen in a fearful indecisiveness. Henri and Elena were the only two children and their companionship and the fact that they simply accepted things for what they were, even mysteries good and bad, kept them insulated. They lived in a bubble. Like everyone else they had no answers but then again they weren't quite sure what the questions were; they just had each other, and in that relationship their time and memories were not as focused on the big picture of what had happened and what would happen, but simply on being together.

Through a combination of gestures, facial expressions, some silly miming, and writing on her board Elena was able to tell the short story of her life and communicate how that for some unknown reason her mother was never happy. She admitted she never knew her father and that she had learned early on to never mention him to her mother. Elena never understood the reason for the depth of her mother's well of sorrow but she felt as if she was somehow linked to it like the bucket that draws from it. She would not talk for long about her mother because it inevitable brought her to the brink of tears, causing her to quickly change the subject and try to lighten the mood.

For the others on the bus the time spent seemed intolerably long but for Henri and Elena the days felt like they quickly sped by, partly because it took Elena longer to tell her tale, but also because they were having fun together. It was odd and enviable for the others to see the two children having so much fun, with Henri occasionally laughing out loud over some silly drawing from Elena or her attempt to mime a chicken.

Henri had no problem communicating with Elena. He seemed to have an unlimited warehouse of stories which he told with enthusiasm. More than once, in spite of the stillness of the bus, Elena would find herself convulsed in silent laughter, tears running down her cheeks, such as when Henri finished one story with "and then Mrs. Green opened up her lunch box and the frog jumped out."

At night, Henri would tell Elena stories about the father he had only heard about. Stories about fighting in a war somewhere and doing great exploits. He admitted that they had become exaggerated over time but Henri loved them and Elena said she enjoyed hearing them and that she wished she could have met him. Henri would usually fall asleep before Elena, the photograph of his father between his fingers, and Elena would take the photograph and slip it quietly back into Henri's shirt pocket as he curled up on the seat across the aisle.

Henri's uncle had moved up to the seat behind the two to act as a barrier due to the visitor who had suddenly appeared at the back of the bus. The visitor sat unmovable, never saying anything. The fact that he had no eyelids was unnerving. It was hard to tell if he was awake, or asleep, or even alive. An air of uncertainty hung over the bus and the only relief for Henri and Elena was each other's company. Elena had made Henri promise that he would not leave. She did not have to worry for it seemed Henri had no choice in the matter.

By the third night most of the passengers had decided to leave the bus. No one did it with either the bravado of the business man or the quiet confidence of the elderly couple. Simply put, the inside of the bus and the outside of the bus presented them with an intolerable situation and in the end they decided that it was better to go with what they did not know then to endure what they did know. Those that left during the day had done so almost in a rushed state of abandonment, like diving off a cliff into the water but without the silly grin. No one was certain how those at night had left since the rest were in a zombie like sleep. Aside from the unusual experience of not feeling any sense of hunger or thirst, their deep sleep was one of the few pleasant experiences the passengers would talk about the next day. One rumor about those leaving at night was that they did not leave but somehow were taken. The reasoning was based on one passenger who braved questioning the frightful man in the back of the bus only to find himself gone the next day.

Late into the night with everyone asleep, Henri woke up with a start. He thought he had heard his name. Maybe it was Elena but she was asleep. He looked back at his uncle who was sitting up with his head back softly snoring. At the back of the bus sat the visitor, his head forward and his eyes still opened. If he noticed Henri looking at him, he did not acknowledge it. Henri turned around and looked to the front of the bus. A man was standing there. He was a young man of about twenty-five. He was tall and thin with light brown hair and blue eyes. Henri recognized his him. It was his father!

"Papa?"

His father smiled warmly and motioned with his hand for Henri to come forward. Henri stood and started walking toward his him. Just as he was about to reach out and touch his hand, his father turned to his left and went down the steps and walked outside. Henri stopped at the top step. His father smiled and waited. Henri was not sure what to do. He turned around and looked at the remaining passengers. They were all soundly sleeping except for the man in the front seat and the visitor in the back. The man in the front seat stared solemnly at Henri.

"How did my father get here?" asked Henri.

The man did not say anything.

His father stood still outside the bus. Henri looked at him. The father waved at him to come toward him. Henri looked at the ground then at his father. Then he turned to the man in the front seat.

"I don't know what to do. I don't understand."

The man in the front seat looked at Henri and smiled.

"It's time to go."

Something about the way the man said it made Henri think of a police officer standing on the street corner directing pedestrians. There was an authority to it that had to be followed. All of the authorities that existed on earth seemed summed up in that man. But it was the authority of someone who knew the right way and was directing others in it. Henri felt that somehow by not going he was breaking the law.

Henri looked back and saw one of Elena's feet hanging out over the seat and into the aisle. A worried look came over his face. Henri had never learned to pray but he had remembered hearing someone once say, "God, help us all if we don't get there on time" when they were hurriedly getting into a cab. He prayed that God would help Elena.

"She'll be okay," said the man in the front seat. "It is not her time. Go!"

That last "go" was as if someone had pushed Henri out of the bus and Henri suddenly was standing on solid ground. He looked up at his father's smiling face. His father reached out to touch Henri's face and as he did so a light fell down on them and his father was engulfed by it and then gone. Henri turned around and the bus was gone too.

The uncle awoke suddenly, early on the fourth day. He was dreaming that he was back in the army on the front lines and had fallen asleep and received a kick to his boot from his commanding officer with the words "wake up soldier. We've a job to do." That physical feeling of being kicked was what woke him. He sat straight up and instinctively lifted his hand to salute but then caught himself, realizing where he was.

He rubbed the sleep from his face and looked up where Henri usually slept. He could see Elena still sleeping, her feet sticking out into the aisle but he could not see Henri. The uncle turned toward the back of the bus and quickly took in the empty seats. In the process he looked at the visitor in the back seat, still sitting quietly, staring straight ahead, the only difference being that there was a slight curl to the visitor's mouth. This creepy, sinister appearance of a faint smile startled him and brought goosebumps to his arms. It was so vague and yet so obvious that the uncle quickly turned away and walked toward the front of the bus, looking hopefully, but fruitlessly at each empty seat, checking if Henri was curled up on one of the seats still sleeping. The closer he got to the door the deeper his heart sank.

The bus driver was so asleep he almost looked unconscious or even dead. The uncle wondered if that was how they all looked at night when they slept. The man in the front seat was leaning against the side of the bus with his feet resting on the seat, his eyes closed but without the same deadened appearance that the other sleepers had.

"He's gone," said the man in the front seat without opening his eyes.

"You let him go?" said the uncle angrily. "How could you?"

"It was his time. It's yours now. Go to him. He needs you." The man continued to keep his eyes shut.

The uncle felt bewildered and stupid. After all the passengers had been through the last few days trying to decide whether to go or stay, here was a man nonchalantly telling him to leave. He felt like a child in school being told to leave the classroom. The man spoke as if he knew what was happening. For the last four days the passengers had been left in a state of indecision and somehow this man seemed to know what was happening.

"Who are you?" asked the uncle.

The man opened his eyes. They seemed to penetrate deep into the uncle.

"I am the Gatekeeper. I am sent here to control who leaves and who returns. It is your time to leave. Hurry! You do not have much time."

The uncle wavered. "Curiouser and curiouser" came the line from the Carroll novel to his mind. Strangeness upon strangeness, mystery upon mystery, evil upon evil, death upon death, beginnings and endings and endings and beginnings he thought. Maybe it was a dream, maybe they were all dead, but which ever one it was, Henri was his charge and if Henri was gone there then there was no point in staying. Everything must come to an end. Perhaps it was his time to find out.

"Go!" commanded the gatekeeper. Instinctively the uncle saluted and was gone.

The uncle stood outside. The sun, even though it was early, pressed upon him. The bus had disappeared and the uncle was standing on the side of the road as cars sped by. It never occurred to him that once someone stepped off the bus that it wasn't they who disappeared but that the bus disappeared and they remained. In the middle of his ponderings a thought forced itself into his mind. Find Henri!

The uncle looked around. How was he to find Henri? He didn't know where to begin and what direction to go. The only thing he could think of was once Henri had left the bus he probably found himself in the same predicament that the uncle was now in. Most likely Henri would try and find his way back home since he didn't know his way to his uncle's house. The uncle crossed the road and tried to flag down a driver. Most of the traffic appeared to be going the opposite way. The uncle could see quizzical faces peering through their car windows at the man in the middle of the desert standing on the other side of the road sticking his thumb out and waving frantically at any cars that passed. They must think I am insane, he thought to himself. "Well, if someone doesn't pick me up, I'll soon be insane from this heat," he said.

Almost as if in response to his words, a truck was seen in the distance approaching the uncle. The uncle stepped a few feet into the road, waving his arms frantically. The driver pulled over and pushed the door open from inside. "What in God's name are you doing out here?" bellowed a large man with curly red hair and a massive bushy beard. The uncle climbed into the truck while the driver swept away the beads of sweat on his forehead.

"I'm not sure what the real story is exactly," replied the uncle. "Let's just say for now that my ride deserted me."

The truck driver grunted but did not press the issue.

"How far are you going?" he asked.

"I'm looking for my nephew. I believe he might be walking on this highway. I'm worried for his safety."

"Is that the last of the stories you're not too sure about?"

"I hope so," sighed the uncle.

"Good. Any other craziness and I would have to get nosey. You seem normal enough. You are normal, aren't you?" The drivers eyebrows raised up so high it looked as if they might touch his hairline.

The uncle peered down the highway. His jaw jutted out.

"I have to find him. He can't last long out here," he answered grimly.

The driver stared at the passenger for a few seconds, then rolled his window down and spit out some tobacco. "Good enough for me," said the driver.

They drove for a few miles and the uncle wondered how far he should go before he considered turning around. The Gatekeeper implied that Henri was in some type of danger and that he needed to hurry. Who was this Gatekeeper? What was a Gatekeeper? The uncle felt he was in new territory with disappearing people, a disappearing bus, and a Gatekeeper. All I need now is a juggling bear and we will have a complete circus, he thought to himself. Wait! What was that on the side of the road?

"Slow down," said the uncle. "I think I see something."

"What in the world!" exclaimed the truck driver. "Someone's passed out on the road. It's a child."

The truck driver pulled over and the uncle jumped out of the truck and ran toward Henri. Henri was unconscious and had burns on his face, neck, and arms. The uncle shook him a little and called his name. Henri's eyes opened a little and that was enough for the uncle.

"Hurry! We need to get him to the hospital."

CHAPTER 14

Decisions

The young girl sat silently and uncomfortably in the back seat of the small car. She was around eight years old. She did not know why she was in the car and where she was being taken. She had soft blue eyes and long black hair that hung over her shoulders. Sitting next to the window she dully observed the flashing images that sped past while she wondered what awaited her next. The rest of the passengers were strangers to her. She had never met them and judging by their behavior she wished that she never had.

"Give me some room, stupid," demanded the boy sitting next to her. There were four children squeezed together tightly in the back. What the boy demanded of the girl was hardly possible, but she tried to move closer to the door.

"She's hogging all the seat," whined the boy to the two adults in the front seat. They were involved in a conversation and ignored him.

"I said, she's hogging all the seat!" screamed the boy at the adults. The woman in the front passenger seat turned around and leaned over the seat. She had stringy dirty hair which was plastered onto a pale bony head. The skin on her face was so tight that it was not hard to imagine what her skull would look like without the skin. Aside from her skeletal appearance she had three distinct features: a hook nose which looked like it had been broken at some time, a thick scar that ran from just below her left earlobe down to the center of her chin, and protrusive eyes that seemed like they could roll out of their sockets at any moment. Her bulging eyes glared at the boy and the scar seemed to redden.

"Shut up and sit still or I'll throw you out the window!"

The boy had heard a lot of abuse in his short life and realized most of it was just empty threats but this woman made it clear that she would fulfill her threat. In her case, he could see that her bite exceeded her bark. The boy cowered and looked away. He slid his hands under his thighs so that no one would see them shaking.

There were two others sitting in the back. On the far side, next to the other window, was another young girl who had her hands clutched tightly together while tears ran quietly down her cheeks. Between her and the boy who had been silenced sat an older boy with oily black hair and scruffs of facial hair poking out between ugly pockmarks scattered on his cheeks. He had a cruel smile on his face and seemed to find the incident with the boy amusing.

The woman in front turned around and spoke to the man. He was her brother and he looked very much like his sister with the exception that his hook nose was not broken and his scars, which were numerous, were hidden under his shirt.

"How much?" she asked.

"I don't know," said the man. "He wouldn't say."

"Well, what are we supposed to do with that?"

"Look," he answered. "We gotta get rid of them, especially the girls. We can't be choosy. We take what we can get. I'm not doing any more time if I can help it."

The woman turned and glared at the four children. Even though the man and she had kept their voices low and spoke in a different language, she wasn't certain if the children might have understood what they were talking about. But the two girls were staring out their windows, the older boy was picking at a scab, and the other boy was looking down, trying not to look too frightened.

The woman reached into her bag and pulled out a cigarette and lighter. "How much farther to the bus station?" she asked as she lit the cigarette. Just as she was bringing the lighter to the end of the cigarette, the car hit a pothole and the lighter dropped out of her hand and landed on her skirt. The skirt started to catch on fire and the woman swore while she tried to put the fire out. The man, distracted by the flame turned toward the woman, veering toward the oncoming traffic. He turned back just in time to see a truck heading straight toward him. The man quickly turned the wheel back toward his lane but it was too hard and too fast. The car flipped sideways and started rolling. There was mayhem in the car as bodies crashed into each other.

The first roll had caused one of the back seat doors to break off and the girl known only as "stupid" to the others flew out and away from the car, landing on a dirt drainage slope away from the road and rolled down the slope into a pile of bushes. She lay there unconscious while the car continued to roll until it came to a stop.

About eight hours later the girl awoke and crawled out of the bushes. She walked up the embankment to the road. The sun was just past setting and there wasn't a car in sight. She was unaware that none of the others had survived and since no one knew she had been in the car, no one would know she had survived. She started walking. She had no idea in which direction she was heading or which direction was best. As night began to creep upon her she followed the white line of the road.

The bus driver awoke shortly after the uncle had left the bus. He yawned and rubbed his hands over his face as if he had risen from a deep sleep, almost as if he had been drugged. Each day since the bus had stopped he had sunk deeper and deeper into a sort of stupor, unable to function, partly from guilt and partly from the mystery of the whole event. It was above and beyond his capacity to grasp and he simply found himself shutting down. He looked in the rear-view mirror and was surprised to find that there were only four remaining on the bus including himself. There was the stranger, Mr. Ward, who somehow seemed no worse for wear than when he had first come on the bus. The mute girl, about two thirds back with her chalkboard around her neck was sleeping. There was also a man in overalls sitting in the back seat, whom he did not remember ever seeing get on the bus. He looked hard at the visitor, wondering why he did not recognize him. The visitor would not meet his eyes and the bus driver felt an odd shiver run up his spine. When and how did so many leave, he wondered. Then he heard a knock on the door to the bus. He stared dumbfounded at the small child who was standing just outside the door.

"Aren't you going to let her in?" asked the stranger.

The bus driver turned to the stranger.

"But-but... How?"

The stranger stood and leaned over the railing and pulled on the handle, opening the door.

"Come in, dear. You must be very tired after such a long walk. Come, let me look at you. How is that bump on your head?"

The girl walked up the steps and it was hard to tell who was more in shock, the girl or the bus driver. The girl looked briefly at the bus driver but was more interested in the stranger. She sat on the seat next to him and laid her head on his shoulder. In no time, she shut her eyes and fell asleep. The stranger easily scooped her up in his arms and moved her to the seat across the aisle, gently laying her down on the seat. He brushed back her hair and gave her bump a light kiss.

"Sleep, Adiya. It will get better. Everything will be better soon."

The stranger sat back down and smiled at the bus driver.

The bus driver, still stunned, managed to sputter.

"How did that happen?"

"What?" answered the stranger. "Do you mean, why is she able to stand outside the bus and not disappear? Do you think that this is some kind of magic bus, or that the air outside is magical air?"

The bus driver leaned his head on the steering wheel.

"I don't know what to think." He paused and added, "You knew her name."

"No," said the stranger. "That is only what I chose to call her. The one for whom she is chosen is free to call her by any name. She is one of the many from her city who were abandoned when born. For years she was raised by various people and organizations, never settling, never knowing who she really belonged with. When she was eight a fire broke out at the house where she was living with many other children. All died but her. She managed to crawl through a window and escape. She blended in with the bystanders and watched as if she were one of them. She was afraid they would blame her for the fire. So she hid at night and roamed the streets during the day. While wandering the streets she was picked up by a couple who specialized in lost children. They would sell them to various parties for various purposes. While travelling, their car overturned and only Adiya survived. She has been walking all night."

"How do you know all of this?" sputtered the bus driver.

"Because I am given the responsibility of restoration. Love has been denied her and I am here to help her find it. Have you not heard the words of the Lord of Glory regarding his little ones that their angels do always behold the Father's face? The time will come when the right person will claim her."

The bus driver looked around the bus, avoiding the dead gaze of the man in back.

"And where have the others gone?" he asked the stranger.

"Their time has come too. I let them go."

"What do you mean, you let them go?"

The gatekeeper spoke to the bus driver as if he were introducing himself for the first time.

"I am here to direct others. I let them in if need be and I let them go when it's time and I stop them if it is not their time. I am the Gatekeeper. I have been the Gatekeeper from before the beginning of time. I was in the garden when it was time for Adam and Eve to leave and I watched so no one would dare come back. I was in Heaven when Satan made a demand for Job. I was there at the tomb when the Master rolled back the stone. I am the Gatekeeper."

If the bus driver had heard something as outlandish as this explanation four days earlier he would have thought that the man was either joking or insane but now that nothing made sense in his world it actually seemed entirely plausible.

"What about these others?" asked the driver. "When is their time?"

"I will know their time when it comes. It has not come yet. But yours has."

The bus driver turned white.

"What do you mean? What happens if I step out there? What happened to the others?"

"It is not always the same," said the Gatekeeper. "And it's not my business. They will either go where they have chosen or where they are needed. As for you, my suspicion is that you have something to do."

The bus driver sat back down on the seat and looked at his hands. They were shaking slightly. He suddenly felt grimy, not from the four days of being in the bus, but from years of running from his sin. There was an active, flowing filthiness in his soul that was filling his pores, soaking his hair, and spilling out onto his skin. It was more than the guilt he had kept locked away. It was his nature. Self-preserving, self-serving, and in the end self-destructive. He had heard a phrase once. He wasn't sure if it was something his mother had said when he was younger or maybe something he had heard in church, but it was "your sin will find you out." Maybe that was what was happening. He could no longer control it. It was finding its way out and in doing so it would find him out. He could feel the stranger looking at him as if he knew something of what was going on.

"I killed a man accidentally some time back," the words tumbled out of his mouth. "I was afraid that I would lose my job or maybe worse go to jail and that I would be unable to care for my mother so I hid the body and car and never told anyone."

He looked down at his hands which were clenched so tightly together that the fingers seemed to mesh together into an unrecognizable tangle of skin, knuckles, and nails. He felt as if he were a wet rag that was being wrung out. Words, thought, truth, lies, life and death were being squeezed out of his worthless, cowardly soul. He dared not look the Gatekeeper in the eyes. There was a long pause with no sense of awkwardness to either the Gatekeeper or the bus driver, but to the visitor in the back, who in spite of his appearance of not paying attention, was painfully listening to every word.

The bus driver cleared his throat. For the first time in days he yearned for some water.

"Actually, the reasons I gave are not true," he stuttered. "I have been telling myself that for years because it helps me live with what I see. The truth is that there is nothing noble in what I did."

The bus driver looked out the window down the desolate highway that seemed to go on forever. There was nothing out there but a man buried in a car. What was it his mother had once told him? It was a saying or phrase she would sometimes repeat but he could not remember it. He felt it was something that might have helped him, or maybe even saved him, but for the life of him he couldn't recall it.

"I was just lost," he continued. "I did not want to do the right thing because I did not want to be found out."

The bus driver closed his eyes and breathed out. He felt a little better just telling someone about the weight he had carried for so many years.

"This whole thing is my fault," he continued. "His presence haunts me. Sometimes he is covered in dirt, a figure encased in the ground I buried him in. Only his eyes are visible. Always visible and always looking at me and through me, wondering what will I do. Other times he appears before me just as he was when I hit him. In his brown suit looking at me with the same innocent expression he had before I hit him. The night we went off the road I saw him like that and tried to swerve out of the way." The bus driver looked up at the Gatekeeper. "I have been dodging ghosts ever since." He looked back toward the nearly empty bus. "And now others are paying the price for it."

The Gatekeeper sat still, enjoying grace and truth before speaking.

"I only know who leaves and who stays and when it's their time, so I don't know what awaits you when you go, but I sense from what has been happening that you are not the main reason we are here. For everyone here there is a reason and the events exist for an outcome to suit them. However, my instincts and experience tell me that the One who orchestrates all things has a greater purpose. You are the vehicle for why we are here. Either way, it is time for you to go now. The others cannot go until you go."

"Will it hurt when I step off?"

The Gatekeeper said nothing.

The bus driver stood and put his hand on the rail as he took his first step. He looked one last time at the Gatekeeper.

"I suppose if it does hurt, I deserve it. What is God like?"

The Gatekeeper remembered that awful day in the garden when he had closed the gates. He had seen for the first time what shame, fear, and humiliation looked like on the face of man. Even then, even before then, there had been a plan to restore a wrong. He smiled warmly toward the bus driver, who like many before him had that same look of man on his face.

"His mercy triumphs over judgement."

The bus driver stepped off the bus expecting the worst of all his fears. Instead, he found himself standing in front of the bus as if nothing extraordinary had happened.

CHAPTER 15

One Life in the Day of Henri

Henri slept fitfully off and on for the next five days. He had heatstroke from his walk under the burning sun, but he also had nearly burst his appendix. The two men had gotten Henri to a hospital just in time. The uncle said nothing to the truck driver other than that Henri was his nephew and had wandered off a bus they were taking. The truck driver was not only a fast driver but he was an expert at being discreet and did not ask any questions. He would however add it to his repertoire of stories to be told next time he was at the Pie'N'Ride Diner with his fellow truckers. Good yarns, embellished over time, were almost as good as the apple pie.

When Henri was feeling better his uncle tentatively asked him what he remembered about the bus ride. All Henri could remember was boarding the bus with his uncle, falling asleep one night and then waking up in a hospital room. The uncle told Henri that the bus had broken down, which was true enough, and that they had walked until someone was able to give them a lift. He wondered if Henri's memory would come back but it never did. The uncle thought it best to leave well enough alone. What could he tell him anyway? That people stepped off a bus and disappeared but that Henri and he did not disappear. It sounded like something a child would make up. Besides, the mystery of why a child should lose both his parents was enough. There was no need to burden him with another.

Once Henri recovered he moved in with his uncle at his home. Henri grew up. He went to school, made friends, played sports, enjoyed hobbies, goofed off, got into trouble sometimes, bought a car, worked various jobs, and dated. Like a light switch, his life went from one of instability to one of stability. His uncle loved him and treated him like a son and Henri loved and honored him as if he were his father.

The farm his uncle owned was small compared to some of the surrounding farms but it was perfect for what the uncle had wanted. He had worked at a desk for the government patent office until he could no longer stand the indoors or the hours and decided to buy the farm and try to live as much off his limited savings, meager disability military pension, and the land as possible. He had a small garden, a few chickens, a couple of cows and two horses. Henri loved the farm. The one hobby the two shared together passionately was their love of horses and horse racing. Henri would read about the history of famous horses and horse racing and the two would listen enthralled to every horse race broadcast over the radio. He loved to memorize statistics on the best races and the best horses.

When Henri was in high school he developed an interest in taxidermy as a result of his biology classes. This evolved into an interest in veterinarian work. Henri would spend his free afternoons and weekends helping the local veterinarian with everything from visiting farms to assisting with surgery. Watching the surgeries led Henri to become fascinated with how things worked and how things healed. By the time Henri had graduated, his desire to help had extended to people. With his high grades, frugal savings from odd jobs, and the help of his uncle, Henri made it into a university where he could study medicine. In time he became a surgeon.

The years rolled on. Henri loved his work, developed a reputation as an excellent surgeon, and enjoyed a quiet life in the same town where had he grown up. He spent the summers at the same lake his uncle would take him to when he was a child and commuted to the city for work. In spite of his medical skills, there was nothing Henri could do for his uncle when he developed terminal cancer except watch him slowly waste away. Henri read to him from his uncle's worn Bible which seemed to give his uncle a measure of comfort. Henri had faithfully gone to church with his uncle while growing up, but his uncle knew that Henri was honoring him and not the one whom the service was about. Henri, though he loved his uncle deeply, simply did not see much use for "church stuff." When the uncle died he left everything to Henri including the Bible he constantly left by his side. Out of respect Henri always kept the Bible on an end table in his apartment but never opened it. After his uncle died Henri realized that living in the town without his uncle just wasn't the same and so he took up a lucrative offer from a prestigious hospital many miles away and bought a penthouse apartment with a beautiful view of the city.

Henri never married. He would tell his friends that he just felt the right one had never come along and besides, it was unfair to ask anyone to try and share their time with someone who worked as many hours as he did. A coworker, who was a camera enthusiast, gave Henri a camera one year for his birthday and from that day on Henri developed a love for photography. He would often spend his free time exploring out of the way places, taking photographs, and then coming back home to develop them in a darkroom he had built in his apartment.

Late one night, Henri was sitting comfortably in a chair in his apartment looking at a proof sheet from a roll of film he had shot a few days earlier. He would often spend his free time walking down some of the lonelier back streets of the city, shooting the scenery of empty back alleys, catching some of the feeling of hopes and dreams deferred or lost, such as a broken baby carriage dangling from a fire escape or a grease covered recycled bin filled with everything but recyclables. Henri found that the best shots were either in early morning or toward sunset. He always felt that the mornings gave a false sense of new beginnings and possibilities while the evenings revealed a tragic lost conclusion. Sometimes a friend would see some of Henri's photographs and comment on how dark they were. Henri never saw them as dark. Instead, they seemed to him to represent the mismanagement of life and the passivity that accompanied it. They were the type of things that no one could explain because time had passed and all interest had been lost, such as the baby carriage on the fire escape or the recycled bin holding a bowling ball split in half. These items had once been new, fresh off the factory line. Their owners at the time were also new in a sense. There was a sense of excitement about what they owned and what they might do. Now, it was all broken and forgotten.

It also occurred to Henri that maybe the people who possessed the random items he found so fascinating had been broken long before they came across these abandoned purchases. Maybe the baby carriage represented an attempt to keep a failed relationship together. The bowling ball was once someone's hobby. Henri's hobby was photograph. Did he take pictures because he was missing something or because he lacked nothing? Henri liked the streets because they made him wonder. Everything owned had at one time represented either joy or hope. Every broken object seem to point back to a broken human, which is perhaps why he had become a surgeon as it gave him the ability to fix someone before they became too lost, too forgotten, and too broken.

As Henri scanned the small rectangular images, deciding on which ones he might want to enlarge, he saw a photograph of a young girl sitting on a discarded bus seat. Henri liked taking portraits when possible, but most of the time the alleys were deserted or the subjects were unwilling to have their pictures taken, so he was surprised to see a picture he did not remember taking. He did, however, remember walking between two large tenement buildings and seeing an abandoned bus seat between the dented trash bins, an object which caught his eye because it was so out of place and seemed to capture the loneliness and absurdity of the alley way. It was very odd, because while Henri had occasionally seen homeless people sleeping on trashed sofas he knew he would remember if he had seen a child sitting upright on a bus seat. He pulled out his magnifying glass and looked closer. It was indeed a picture of a young girl sitting on a bus seat as if it were a normal day on the bus and she had been travelling. She had dark hair and a dress that looked like it was from an earlier time. Around her neck was a string which held a small chalkboard. Henri held the photograph up close to the light by his chair. He picked up a pair of reading glasses and along with his magnifying glass tried to get a better look at what was written on the chalkboard.

"Henri—help!"

Henri woke up about an hour later with a nice little bump on his head from hitting the coffee table after he fainted. He went to the bathroom and washed his face and hands and took a look at the bump that, though while sore, wasn't bleeding. Henri went back to the chair and looked at the proof sheet again, using his magnifying glass to scan it, gently rubbing around the bump on his forehead as he moved the glass over the pictures. It was Elena. The frightened face he had completely forgotten looked exactly the same as he now remembered it. The dress, the chalkboard, the seat, passengers, and bus came clearly back into Henri's memory as if he had just reseated himself in the bus. Then the rest came back, the disappearance of the passengers, the strange man who had suddenly appeared on the bus, and his uncle.

Henri sat back in his chair and rested the glass and proof sheet on his legs. Why hadn't his uncle told him any of this, he asked himself. Why didn't he tell Henri that they needed to go back and help? He sat and mulled this over for a while. He realized these were the questions a child would ask. His uncle was an adult who had to take care of a young boy who was not his. He could see now, from an adult's view, that his uncle was simply being practical and trying to take care of Henri, not to mention that from an adult point of view the whole thing seemed too fantastic and it was probably just easier to leave it behind. Still, Henri would like to know what had happened, but even more importantly, what was happening now.

Henri stood and went to the desk where he had placed the recent negatives he had developed. They were in individual plastic sheets in strips. He sat back down and held them up to the lamp light next to his chair and followed the pictures along each row of negatives until he found the section of the alley which he remembered taking the picture of the bus seat. His eyes scanned past miniature photos of graffiti painted walls, boarded doorways, and trash bins until he saw the negative of the bus seat. The seat was empty, just as he had remembered. He looked back at the proof sheet he had developed in his darkroom from the negatives and there was Elena sitting on the seat looking at him plaintively.

"Why is it on the print sheet but not on the negative?" he said aloud.

Henri grabbed the negatives and almost jumped out of his seat, heading toward his darkroom. He quickly set up his equipment and made a larger print of the negative only to see it come up without Elena in the photo. It appeared the only evidence he had was the proof sheet. He went back and looked at it again through the magnifying glass. It was still there. The whole thing made no sense, he thought to himself. If I can print it out as a negative, then why can't I enlarge it? He grabbed one of his digital cameras and took a picture of the proof sheet to see if it would show Elena on the bus. Just like the darkroom, all it showed was the seat.

Henri sat for almost an hour trying to resolve in his mind why Elena would only show up on the print sheet. There was no answer, he reasoned, and maybe he was just asking the wrong questions.

It had been so long ago, he thought. Why would all of this come back to him when it was too late to do anything about it? He thought of his promise to Elena not to leave her alone on the bus. How terrified she must have been when she woke up and noticed he was gone, especially when that horrid looking man had appeared on the bus. He recalled the look on her face when she realized her mother was gone. She was a frightened little girl and he was a boy trying to be brave. A brave boy who left. Why did he leave? Of all the events which were pouring into his consciousness the one detail he could not recall was why or how he had left.

Henri felt he had to do something. It certainly seemed impossible to believe that Elena and the bus were where he had left them. In all likelihood everyone on the bus was probably dead. Henri kept looking back at the proof sheet just to verify that Elena was still there but even if she had suddenly disappeared from the proof sheet, he knew it did not matter because now he remembered and that changed everything. If it did come back to him for a reason then he had to try and find out why, plus it irritated him that he did not know why he had left. At the very least he felt he should drive out to the place where the bus had broken down and go from there. If nothing happened then he would simply come back home. Hopefully after all of these years he could find it.

It took a few days for Henri to arrange his affairs. He told his practice and his friends that he would be vacationing for an indeterminate time. He packed the essentials, emptied his safe of his emergency money and got into his car and drove. After looking at a map, he thought he located which road he thought the station would be on and that it would take about six to eight hours to reach it. He remembered that his uncle had commented while they were on the bus that a newer highway ran parallel to the old one and that eventually the old one would hardly be used. As he drove, the memory of a gas station with a large rock in front came to his mind. He reasoned that the gas station would either be abandoned or gone by now but perhaps the rock would still be there.

On the road Henri thought of Elena. If by some crazy chance that she was alive and he found some way of locating her, she would be as old as he. Had she stepped off the bus and disappeared like the others? But then, Henri and his uncle had stepped off and not disappeared. Henri wondered what had happened to the others. Perhaps some, like him, had simply walked down the road until someone had picked them up.

While Henri drove, the ridiculousness of what he was doing almost overwhelmed him. A few times he nearly turned around and headed back home. The sun was beginning to set and Henri knew that if he did not see something soon he would have to find a place to spend the night and come back the next day. As he came over a slight crest he noticed a car pulled over on the side of the road. A man was walking from some bushes that were a few feet away from the road toward the car. About twenty yards further down the road was a bus. Henri pulled over just behind the car and got out. The man stopped and looked at Henri. He had a strained look on his face. It was the bus driver.

CHAPTER 16

Hell and Heaven

The mother sat on the rock and waited, alternating her gaze from the stranger to Elena then to the creature, who filled her with revulsion and hate, and then back to Elena. Kay could not tell whether the time had been an hour or a century. She was reminded of when people used the expression "it felt like eternity" because when they used the word eternity they were really referring to an extended period of time but she was seeing that there was no sense of time in eternity. It simply was. A second was no different than an hour, an hour was no different than a year, and a day was no different than a thousand years. Thought on the other hand felt in some way chronological or maybe linear was a better word.

She had one thought on her mind and that was her daughter's welfare. However even that single thought went from one point to another, expanding into extended thought and contracting back into a single concentration, or even a single word, Elena. Like an accordion with air going in and out, the thought of Elena would expand and contract. She would imagine what life might be like should they ever get through this together. Where would they live? What type of woman would Elena grow into? Would she marry? Who was the boy on the bus? Did Elena like him? What did Elena like? What was Elena like?

After years of pushing Elena to the farthest corner of her mind, she now felt that she would never weary of thinking about her, a fact which caused her to realize it was probably the first time that she had ever experienced joyful contentment or genuine love. There were times in the past when Kay thought she was content. Looking back she knew she was just busy with activities that amused her and mistook fun for contentment. Kay had thought she was in love once but now realized that her marriage was just another busy activity keeping her soul occupied. Time may have been able to change that but it would also have had to change her. And what about her husband? He had been busy too. Probably in his mind, his infidelity was as innocuous as her shopping for new shoes. Just something to do and who could say that she would not have done the same in time. Kay had always been selfish and flighty. Even when their marriage was at its best there was no foundation like the rock she was sitting on. Until now, she would never have been able to quietly sit and patiently wait.

She thought of the man who had raped her. The Toad was a beast who loved not just having woman but crushing them. He took delight in other women's pain. In prison many of the women would tell their fantasies about how they would kill him if given the chance. It was a hobby for those not yet afflicted by his sadistic behavior, a cathartic experience for others, and a potential reality for those who had been most painfully hurt and had the least to lose. At the very least it was a diversion from the routine and boredom. At times it reminded her of the shallow joy she and her rich friends experienced in their social gatherings, gossiping and back biting each other. There was a love there too, but not for others. Kay thought of the love her parents had for her and how hurt they had been when she was sent to prison. It had hurt her father's standing in the community and with his business associates. He had to distance himself from her to maintain proper connections. She remembered the last time he visited her in prison and with lowered eyes told her that she would have some money when she was released but that he could not continue to visit her. Kay knew her parents loved her but even then it was a love with limitations.

Because of the pain she felt, she had not only limited her love with Elena but had cut it off by emotionally distancing herself. She had closed herself off to her because of the door to anger which she feared would open should she not be able to control herself.

Elena loved her. Kay could see it when Elena looked at her. She could not figure out why Elena loved her after the way she had been ignored. Maybe pure, unlimited love was like that she thought. It could not be figured out and it could not be dissuaded. Or maybe it could. How long would it take to crush Elena's love for her?

It would never happen again, the mother vowed. Not if she was given a second opportunity. Occasionally the mother would go up to the bus and look in. No one ever seemed to notice her. Once she thought she saw a man at the back of the bus look at her but she could not be sure. *If I have to wait throughout eternity I will*, she thought.

At some point, Kay saw a large woman get off the bus. She had an angry look and way about her. It reminded Kay of when she was little and she heard her mother refer to a certain woman as a brawler. This woman looked like a brawler. She looked like she wanted to fight. Kay watched her as she stepped off the bus with her hands clenched and her jaw set firm. The brawler looked to the left and to the right. She looked right at Kay but gave no indication of seeing her. The brawler took a few steps away from the bus and stopped. Suddenly her countenance changed drastically. She went from anger to surprise to a state of abject fear. She fell to her knees and began to plead with words so mingled with tears and fear that is was unintelligible. A dark cloud fell over the brawler. The brawler, looking in all directions for some relief, this time saw Kay and the terror in her eyes met the eyes of the mother. The brawler tried to speak while desperately reaching her hand to the mother. Then the cloud closed around her and she was gone.

The air seemed to be filled with judgement, not judgement as an act or decision, but judgement as a person. Kay could feel it all around her. The ability of someone who ultimately knew what was right and what was wrong. It was the voice she first heard shortly after leaving the bus when she had screamed into the night air. This voice had judged the brawler. This was the voice that had judged the men and woman who had hurt her in her life. This voice was now judging her as she reasoned about love. This voice was love and this voice was judgement. Why had the cloud not surrounded her, the mother wondered. The brawler woman had an ugly, hating look about her as if she were quite use to it. The mother knew in her heart that she was not that much different. She had been ugly all her life. She deserved the cloud too. Why had it not come for her? Kay prayed her second prayer to a God she did not know, prayed that He would give her time to help Elena before she was swept up by the cloud.

She waited. A man wearing a business suit stepped off the bus. He too looked around. He looked at his watch. Then he tapped it and looked at it again. Then he took the watch off and put it to his ear. Irritated, he turned around to face the bus and froze. He walked forward a few steps and reached out his hands. Kay realized that the man could not see the bus. There was a strange look of panic and for a while she watched the man as he stood shaking. After some time he seemed to compose himself and looked up and down the highway. He lifted one of his hands as if to flag down a car and walked straight through where the bus would have been. She saw the man walk a few steps and then he disappeared into the haze. The bus was still there.

Kay watched others get off the bus and have somewhat the same experience as the man in the business suit. They were surprised that the bus had disappeared and then eventually found their way across the road and presumably found a ride. She was not sure. She could hear the sound of cars but could not see anything other than the gray haze which seemed to thicken the further out it went. The mother was alone, unseen, unknown, and probably for the most part unwanted. Except for Elena she thought.

Then an older couple stepped off the bus. They behaved much differently than the others who had departed. The most noticeable thing about them was their countenance. Before they even stepped onto the ground it was apparent that they had great joy. The look on their faces reminded her of her friends' faces when she was a child and they would run into the lake at her grandfather's house.

The older couple did not look around at the bus. They did not seem to care whether it was there or not. Their gaze seemed to be fixed on something that Kay could not see. Slowly, the air became brighter and brighter. Normally Kay would have shielded her eyes under such brightness but for some reason it did not hinder her from viewing what was happening. She realized at some point that the brightness was something different than the normal brightness that comes from the sun. It was a brightness that made everything clearer. She could see the rapturous look of joy on the elder couple's face. They could not really be called elderly anymore. They did not appear to have a specific age. The only way she could describe it even though she wasn't sure what she meant by it was that they looked eternal. They laughed and it felt that all that was around her laughed also, almost as if it would have been a sin not to laugh. Kay was laughing too, completely caught up in joy. She had always thought of laughter as being associated with humor but now she realized humor was simply a by-product of joy. The idea of God having a sense of humor now seemed completely backward. Humor was found in joy and joy was found in God. It was people who only had a sense. They had only touched the edges of the glory it revealed. Even then, it was often polluted and perverted. He was pure humor because He was pure joy.

A sudden silence fell over everyone. There was a feeling of anticipation. Kay felt that someone was approaching and all of creation was standing respectfully at attention. Then she felt Him. She could not see anything but she knew He was there. His presence was unmistakable. She remembered as a child hearing the words from a hymn "Lord of Lord and King of Kings" being sung and now knew what they meant. She heard voices singing and even though she could not distinguish the words she knew that they were words of praise. Kay fell onto her face and worshipped. She did not think whether she was worthy or not, she simply knew that it was impossible not to worship.

There was no sense of time, of a beginning, a middle, or end. Kay felt that this could continue for all of eternity and she would be content. She was not even anxious for Elena's sake. Worship demanded and gave patience. However, she sensed that at some point that it had ceased and that things had returned to what they were. She slowly lifted her head off the ground and looked up. There He was crouched down looking at her. She looked at His face. There was a look of mirth on his face. He seemed to be enjoying the moment. He looked as if He enjoyed everything. "Catherine," was all he said.

Catherine was struck with how rugged his face was. She had a picture of Jesus on a wall growing up and she always felt that he looked almost frail with his long hair and robe, and hand held up slightly. She had often thought of Him as one dimensional but she realized that this face contained everything in it. She could look upon that face for eternity and never feel that she had seen it completely.

He reached out his hand and she took it and as she did Catherine felt the roughness of the nail scar in his hand. She looked down at his hand and realized that all her life she had lived with pettiness and selfishness. Every grievance, every grudge, every hurt she could think of stemmed from a grubby pettiness. She felt ashamed but realized that the scar in His hand had wiped all that away. Then she saw the hurt that had been caused toward her, first by her husband, then her friends, her father's turning away, and even the cruel actions of the jailer. The scars were there for them too and if she could not forgive them then she felt that she would find herself betraying what the scars were. Catherine fell to her knees and wept. Waves of love washed over her as she worshipped.

As Catherine worshipped there was a growing awareness that someone was in need. She opened her eyes and lifted her head to find that everything was black around her and that the bus was no longer visible. In front of her, on the rock, was a small empty glass. She heard a faint groan to her left and as she looked a dim pathway of light opened up like a trail leading in the direction of the new highway. She clasped the cup and stood. Catherine was unsure of how she could help but she knew that she was being offered the opportunity to serve in some capacity and that the offer was free from any sense of obligation but was a test in sorts of sacrificial love. There was a feeling that a price would be paid but she did not know what exactly it would be. If she chose not to follow through she would still be loved but she would not have loved in return.

She could see at the end of the lighted tunnel the business man whom she had seen earlier get off the bus and head in the direction of the highway. He appeared to be lying on the ground in pain. Catherine made her decision and took a step toward the man. The moment she did the thick blackness was gone and she was in the desert in the middle of the day with the blistering sun beating down. The bus was gone.

A shot of fear ripped through her as she wondered where Elena was now. She took a step back toward the rock and was instantly enveloped back into the black covering, the bus back in its place. She stood still vacillating between the two worlds. It seemed that when she had finally come to a place where she recognized who she was and what Elena was to her she was being asked to choose between Elena and the one who had given her Elena. She didn't know whether she would ever see Elena again if she helped this stranger and yet the one who had touched her was asking her to take a risk and make a sacrifice to help him. She cried out in agony. Then a verse she must have heard many years ago, long forgotten, came to her, "*if be possible, let this cup pass from me. Nevertheless not my will but thine be done.*" It strengthened the mother and she committed Elena to her master and started toward the man.

The heat from the sun poured down, this time feeling much hotter than before, almost as if it was challenging her, mocking her, and demanding her to turn around. For a moment she paused, struck by its sheer force and wondered if she could make it to the man. There is only one way to find out she thought to herself and pressed forward. Though the distance appeared not more than a couple of hundred yards each step was arduous and her legs ached as she walked. She remembered that the man had walked strangely, apparently with some type of walking disability. She looked down at her legs as she moved. They seemed fine but it was clear that every step brought a paralyzing pain that shot down from her hips to her toes. The sun bore down and within a minute she was drenched in sweat, her skin on fire and her throat closing up, feeling unspeakably dry.

At the halfway point, she collapsed to the ground and cried out in pain. She looked at the man, still not moving. Why had no one stopped she wondered. Then she saw. Like a motion pictured played out in front of her she saw what had happened to the man. He had been hobbling along excitedly toward a car of young men who were waving him toward them. Once he reached the car the men got out and surrounded him. She saw the man attacked as the men beat him and take his wallet. She saw him attempt to fight back, doing his best to defend himself but was eventually overcome by their strength and numbers. She saw them drive off and heard their cruel laughter through the window, across the great expanse of time and space. She knew that laughter had also reached her Masters ear. Catherine stood, set her focus on the man and took another step.

She finally reached the man and knelt down beside him and lifted his head and rested it on her lap. The cup had grown cool in her hand and she saw that it was filled with water. Her throat was closed and the water looked so inviting. Take a little sip, she thought to herself. You have come a long way. You deserve it. One sip. There will still be some left for him.

"Be quiet!" she commanded the air.

Catherine gently gave the man some sips from the glass. She thought she could hear faint singing in the background but she could not be sure. She tried to say something to the man but her mouth was too dry. The man revived a little and looked at her through the slits of his swollen eyes. The woman gently laid the man's head back down and tried to stand but passed out instead.

When Catherine awoke she was back on the rock facing the bus.

CHAPTER 17

Repair

One reason the bus driver had decided to step off the bus was because he thought that by doing so he might lift whatever curse had been put on the bus. In spite of the fact that he had spent much of his last few days in a foggy stupor he was aware these sentiments were shared and whispered by others on the bus. He had a faint remembrance of a Sunday School story about a man named Jonah who allowed himself to be thrown off a ship so that a storm would stop and the other passengers would survive. He could not remember the rest of the story, except that afterward the seas calmed and Jonah was swallowed by a whale. For the bus driver, being thrown off the bus felt as if he was being thrown into a sea of uncertainty. Surely he would be judged for what he had done. He deserved it. How that judgement would come was what terrified him.

The first thing that he did once he stepped off the bus was to do what most of the other departing passengers had done. He turned around. In the bus driver's case however, the bus was still visible. The bus driver almost jumped up and down with excitement. He pushed on the center of the door and it opened without any difficulty. Still a little cautious or maybe superstitious, he only put one foot on a step and kept one on the ground while he twisted his neck to look up at the stranger in the front seat.

"Hey," he yelled. "It's okay. I'm still here."

No one answered and so the bus driver stepped back outside and looked up at the window where the stranger had been seated. He pounded on the window and yelled. Not only did no one answer but no one was there. The driver stepped back to get a better look inside but it was clear that no one was inside the bus. Something felt wrong about the bus, not only the bus but the time of day. The driver had been so focused on what might happen when he stepped off the bus and was so elated that he was not only alive but that the bus was still there. In the excitement he failed to notice that it was now early evening instead of morning. And there was one other major difference. This was not the same bus.

It was a Transit Plus bus and very similar to the one he had been driving yet it looked older and newer at the same time. The logo on the side of the bus seemed sharper with a fresher paint job yet the bus looked like an older model. He decided to examine the back tire that had blown out. He walked toward the back of the bus and squatted down to take a closer look. Not only had all the passengers heard the noise of the tire popping when they had pulled over, but the back end of the bus had lowered from the flat. There was no doubt that the tire had blown. But as he rolled his hand over the tire he could not find any sign of a puncture or even of any significant wear. He closed his eyes, rubbed his face, and sat down on the ground. He felt a cool breeze blow on the back of his neck. He opened his eyes. The air felt different, almost like autumn.

He stood and looked around. Everything felt different and yet something felt similar. That was when he noticed for the first time a car about twenty yards behind the bus pulled over to the side of the road. *Why didn't I see that before?* he asked himself.

He walked toward the car. There was a familiarity about the color and make that reminded him of something but he couldn't think what it was. The emergency lights were flashing and the driver's side door was open but there was no one in sight. He stopped and turned slowly, looking at the desert, the newer highway, and back at his bus. Something was not right. He turned around and looked back at the car. Then, it was as if every memory he had tried to suppress came crashing through and without any doubt it was clear to him. It was the dead man's car.

It was not only his car but it was the time and place of the accident. It was not a dream or a vision, or even a visitation of the man, but it was the real physical place just moments after he had hit the driver nearly a decade earlier. The bus driver started to tremble. This was his judgement. This was his punishment. Of all the ways to suffer for his sin he could never have conceived of this. Physical torture and pain would have been more endurable. His soul pleaded with the dealer of judgement. Let me die a thousand hellish deaths, but do not make me relive this moment.

He stood, paralyzed by the turn of events. The desert too was paralyzed, as if every living thing was waiting to see what he would do. To live in an endless loop of the grotesque crime against this man seemed unbearable. The bus driver fell to his knees and groaned. It was a greater hell than he could bear. Then a surprisingly wonderful thing happened. He had a thought. A beautifully redemptive idea grew, like a flower in the desert, amidst the fear and torment. Maybe he was being given a chance to do the right thing. Even if it did not change the reality of what had happened, it still gave him an opportunity to not feel ashamed. He had been a coward and a destroyer. Without wanting to admit it, he always knew that the real wrong was not that he had killed the man but that he had covered it up. As much pain as accidentally killing the man would bring to those who loved him, he was always painfully conscious that keeping that information from them must have been much worse. That would be a grief that could torment someone their entire life.

Once, when he was young, he accidentally broke a vase and was too embarrassed and frightened to tell his mother. She found out as mother's often do. She said only one thing to him, "Accidents happen, but decisions are made." This was what he had been trying to remember earlier. He knew hitting the man was an accident but his decision to hide it had been his sin. If he could correct that, then he would try now, even if it wasn't real but just a dream or some cruel afterlife exercise in which he would have to face the victim over and over. He went to look at the man.

He found the thick bush where the man was lying, his legs sticking out and an outline of his body partially hidden behind the leaves. He leaned over, paused a moment, and then firmly grabbed the man's ankles, causing his socks to slide down to the top of his shoe. He took a deep breath, pulled the man toward himself, his eyes closed tight and grunting as he did so. The man slid on the dust floor, his clothes catching briefly on pieces of the bush before being pulled away, then bunching up as the ground dragged dirt around and under him. The driver had closed his eyes as a reflex when pulling on the body but when the body had cleared the bus he realized that he was reluctant to open them. That face would be waiting. He set the man's legs down and rubbed his hands over his face, silently encouraging himself before opening them. He was surprised to see that the man's face did not seem to have that same haunting look to it as it did before, but appeared to be almost encouraging. The bus driver decided that he would try and take him to the hospital and deal with the consequences. He would admit everything. It had been an accident that he could not change, but he could correct what happened next.

He wrapped his hands around the wrists of the man and pulled him into a sitting position, then leaned down and pulled him up and over his right shoulder. The body was dead weight and the bus driver was unsure if he would be able to lift him, but after some wiggling and squirming with the body he was able to stand with the man firmly planted on his shoulder. When he got to the car he did the whole process in reverse and as gently as he could he placed the man down, leaning against the front passenger door so that he could unopen the back door with the intention of laying the man down on the long single vinyl back seat. It was then he remembered he could not use the man's car because of the flat tires. He would have to carry him in the bus.

The bus driver had unopened the back door and was leaning over the man trying to think of the best way to place him in the bus when he heard a car pull up behind him. While his mind raced like an accelerated pinball machine it felt as if his heart had stopped and the blood in his body had ceased circulating. This was the last thing he had anticipated especially since the first time this had happened he had what he thought was the good fortune to not be seen by anyone. It was confusing too because if he were being given a chance to do the right thing then why were the circumstances changing? It seemed unfair to be put in this position. He had made a decision to do the right thing by taking the man to the hospital and confessing that he had hit him with the bus. Now he was being misdirected. Now he would have to confess to a random stranger.

"I suppose in the end it doesn't really matter," he said quietly with resignation to himself.

He stood slowly and faced the car which now had come to a stop behind him. The headlights were on when the car pulled up and the bus driver put his hand up to block the glare. The driver, realizing that his lights were in the bus driver's face, turned them off, then opened his door and stepped out. He was an older man, dressed casually, but it was obvious to the bus driver that the man had a refined taste in clothes. He was also driving a style of automobile that the bus driver had never seen.

The man walked toward the bus driver. It took the man only a moment to notice the bus up ahead, the bus driver's uniform and the deep strain on the bus driver's face to get some idea that something either had gone wrong or that something wrong was being done. There was a feel in the air that things were off. He walked toward the bus driver. When he got within a few feet he stopped and stared oddly at the bus driver. The bus driver had the queer sensation that the man somehow recognized him.

"Is everything all right?" the man asked.

The bus driver's throat felt so dry he was not sure he could get any words out. He was about to say the words he should have said long ago.

"I've hit him," he stammered. "I don't think he's alive. I was going to try and take him to a hospital just in case."

The man then noticed one shoe just sticking out from the side of the car. He quickly moved past the bus driver and around the back of the car toward the front passenger side.

"I'm a doctor," said the man. "Have you checked his pulse? Here, let me look."

Without waiting for any answer from the bus driver, the doctor knelt down and checked the man's wrist. Then he checked his neck.

"It is very faint, but I feel something. He has lost a lot of blood. I have a kit in my trunk. I need to stop some of this bleeding and then we can get him to the hospital."

"He's alive? Will he make it?"

"I don't know," said the doctor. "We'll try."

The doctor did what he could and then together they put the man into the doctor's car. It was a little more cramped than the victim's car but since both his tires were blown and there was no time to patch even one tire, they had to make do the best that they could. After getting directions from the bus driver to the nearest hospital, the doctor said that he would drive the man to the hospital and that the bus driver could follow in his bus. They would come back later with a tow truck to pick up the man's car. After they got the man secured into the doctor's car, the doctor went to the driver's side and opened his door.

"I'll meet you at the hospital," said the doctor. "By the way, my name is Henri."

The doctor gave a short wave and sped off. The bus driver wearily lifted his hand in return as he watched the car move down the road. The bus driver wished that he could drive the man's car instead of his bus to the hospital. He wanted nothing to do with the bus but the doctor had taken the man's keys with him and there was no way to fix both tires. The bus driver trudged to the front of the bus fearful of what he might find inside. Once he entered he realized that he was entering the same bus that he had hit the man with and not the bus with the stranded passengers. It occurred to him that he wasn't sure which bus he really wanted to be in at the moment. He tentatively turned the ignition over and the bus started up without issue. The bus driver felt a sense of relief and a sense of fear. He was grateful that the man was alive but he was worried what this would mean to him and his mother. "Accidents happen," he thought. "And decisions are made." He had been given a second chance, if that was what this was, and he would live with his accident and his decision. He drove to the hospital. When he arrived he found that the man had been admitted by the doctor and was in surgery. The doctor was nowhere to be found. The bus driver was told that the car had been taken care of by a local tow truck company and that a police officer was waiting to take a statement from him.

The bus driver told the police that he had hit the man accidentally and how a doctor had driven by and was able to help. He was nervous but relieved to confess. The police officer took notes and then looked over the bus driver's shoulder and nodded.

"And was she a passenger, or is she with you?" he asked.

The bus driver turned around. Adiya was sitting on a chair against the wall, her palms on the side of the seat and her feet swinging back and forth. She looked at the bus driver and smiled. He realized he had never seen her smile or heard her voice. After a few moments the police officer cleared his throat.

"Sir?"

The bus driver turned back to the police officer.

"Yes, her name is Adiya. She's with me."

CHAPTER 18

The Croaking Toad

Leo, in spite of his constellation and mother's wish, was never a lion, especially after he had started working at the prison. He may have been Bossman to those who worked for him, but to the women at the prison he was always The Toad. His bulbous eyes, bloated body, and the fact that he was universally hated and feared earned him the notorious, yet secret nickname. Only one had ever dared call him that to his face and shortly after that she been found dead in the shower beaten to death. The Toad had indeed grown fat over the years. His flesh was fat and his soul was fat. The rottenness of his bones made it a wonder that he could even stand but he was fed by the lust that constantly drove him. The women at the prison, their terror and anguish, which he was pleased to provide, seasoned his desire and their destruction was the wellspring of his strength. But the Toad was slowing down and judgement was coming.

He had often been accused of suspicious behavior but had some-how managed to dodge any consequences from his actions. It helped that he was not alone. Over time the Toad was responsible for hiring and managing the staff. This allowed him to hire those sympathetic to his devious behavior. Through the years he had built a protective scaffolding of employees who would conspire to protect him while allowing them their own peculiar liberties. However, scapegoats were needed when trouble would occasionally arise. The Toad managed to always keep on staff one or two who could take the blame for any possible maleficence. It wasn't only the female prisoners' lives whose lives he enjoyed crushing. Many an honest man's life was ruined in order to protect the system set up by the Toad.

The downfall of the Toad started one night as the Toad had come home to his empty house. He had cleared out his mother's garden after her death and put a lawn in its place. However, whereas his mother was very attentive and particular regarding her garden, the Toad was the opposite. The lawn often times would go months without any maintenance. Eventually it became an ugly mix of crabgrass and weeds. He was too lazy and indifferent to mow it on his own and too cheap to hire someone regularly. The interior of the house remained the same with the exception of the master bedroom, which was completely renovated. Ever since his father's disappearance the master bedroom had acquired a sickening odor to it. It was so bad that the Toad had everything in the room burned. He replaced the carpet and put up a new coat of paint. He kept the room simple with only a bed, nightstand and chest of drawers. There were no photographs on the nightstand or pictures on the walls. The only thing the Toad was fussy about, which was incongruous to how he kept his lawn, was the habit of neatly making his bed after a night's sleep. This was why he was so startled one night when he came home to find the bed unmade and the pillow on the floor.

The first time it happened, the Toad just stood in his doorway with his jaw opened in disbelief. It was such a strange thing to see because to the Toad there could only be two possibilities, each of which seemed unlikely. One was that he had forgotten to make his bed and left the pillow on the floor. This was out of the question for the Toad. It wasn't even a matter of remembering if he had made the bed that morning. Making the bed was as close to a religious exercise as the Toad had ever practiced. He simply would not, could not forget something like that.

The only other possibility was that someone else had slept in the bed during the day. This produced all sorts of questions such as who, how, and why. First, the Toad considered how. If someone broke in there should be evidence somewhere. The Toad went through the house checking every door, window, and any other possible opening.

In the end he found no windows were broken or doors jimmied. Whoever came was either very good at not leaving signs of illegal entry or had a duplicate key. The Toad had no friends or lovers he could even begin to suspect, so for the moment, the question of how would have to be set aside until further information was available.

The question of who and why was equally baffling. The Toad could think of no one he knew who would do such a thing either as a prank or out of need. None of his coworkers, which were really the only people he had any consistent contact with, would dare do something like this and expect to live. What made it even more perplexing was that it had happened during the day sometime after he had left for work. It would have to be someone who worked at night and needed to sleep during the day.

The Toad decided to do something which for him was quite humbling. He would go to his immediate neighbors and ask if they had seen anyone who appeared suspicious. He went from door to door like a salesman with hat in hand questioning each neighbor if they had seen anyone entering or exiting his house. Most of his neighbors were not eager to see the Toad at their door. Given the Toad's strange family history and his unappealing personality they probably would have preferred the salesman. But out of a dozen houses that the Toad visited, only one commented that they had seen someone go into the Toad's house that day. An elderly lady whom the Toad suspected of senility told him that the only one she saw that morning entering the house was he, himself.

The Toad washed his bedsheets that night before going to sleep. The idea of someone else on his bed annoyed him. And though he would never admit it to anyone, it was also unnerving. That night he slept fitfully and woke up in a foul mood. He dressed, carefully made his bed, and headed to work. As he drove away from the house he looked down side streets and in backyards to see if he could spot anything unusual.

"Horatio!" bellowed the Toad when he walked into his office.

"Horatio! Where is Horatio?" yelled the Toad again even louder.

An office clerk walked into the Toad's office.

"You need something, Bossman?" he asked.

"Are you deaf?" asked the Toad, his eyes bulging. "Where is Horatio?"

"He's changing, Bossman. You want me to get him?"

The Toad glared at the clerk, curious if the window was large enough for him to toss the clerk through and also wondering if he would survive a five floor drop. The clerk got the point and hurried out. A few minutes later, Horatio came through the door, trying to get his breath after running from the changing room, his shirt half-buttoned. It was clear that the clerk had gotten the point and made it clear to Horatio.

"Yes, Bossman. What's wrong?"

The Toad glared at Horatio. "Where did you sleep yesterday when you went home?"

Horatio was caught off guard by the strange question. His eyes furrowed close together while he tried to comprehend the question.

"In my bed?" answered Horatio. He wasn't sure if that was the type of answer the boss wanted.

"Are you asking me?" said the Toad with some sarcasm in his voice.

"No, Bossman, it's just that I wasn't expecting that kind of question. Is that what you meant? Where did I actually sleep?"

The Toad stared at the wall, his jaw working back and forth in the grinding motion he often did when he was thinking.

After a minute Horatio cleared his throat. "Bossman?"

The Toad turned around and set his jaw.

"Find out who worked last night's graveyard shift and where they slept." Horatio thought it was a ridiculous request but he also knew that look on his boss's face. So he decided it was better to get grief from the other men than another one of those looks from his boss.

"Yes, sir, Bossman. You'll have that tomorrow."

"Get it today!" commanded the Toad.

"Okay, Bossman," replied Horatio. It was going to be a long day for Horatio.

While Horatio annoyed his coworkers the Toad found the number of a private eye. He contacted Sampson from The Delmonico

Detective Agency, a.k.a. DDA, a detective that the Toad had used a number of years ago to look for his father. At the time the Toad hired Sampson, he did not care where his father was or if anything had happened to him, but for insurance purposes he had to prove he had made the effort to locate his father. Sampson's work had satisfied the insurance company and the Toad. Sampson had also done some side work for the Toad under the table. Occasionally the Toad had needed help getting either himself out of trouble or someone else in trouble. The Toad and Sampson had a history in which either could burn the other with what they knew; therefore, it was in their best interest to remain loyal.

"DDA. Sampson here. What can I do for you Leo?"

"I need you to watch my house for the next five days from 8:00 AM till I get home, usually around 6:00 PM. I need to know if anyone is breaking into my house."

"Do I need to ask any questions?" said Sampson.

"No, just let me know what you see. Don't wait until the end of the week to call if you see someone. Oh, wait. I'll be out of town for the next two days. If you find anything, call here and leave a message. I want you to just observe. If anyone goes in, follow them when they leave and find out where they live. Do not confront them."

"No problem. Our rates have gone up some since you last used us."

"That's not a problem," replied the Toad.

"Okay, I'll put one of my men on it tomorrow."

"No," said the Toad abruptly. "I want you on it. You do it and I'll pay you double."

There was a pause on the other end of the phone. The Toad could hear muffled sounds. It sounded as if Sampson was talking with someone while his hand was over the mouthpiece. He heard a door shut and then Sampson came back on the phone.

"All right, Leo, I'll move some things around and do it."

"Good," said the Toad and hung up.

The next two nights the Toad spent the night in a hotel in a neighboring city. He had been called as a witness in a murder case. One of the inmates had stabbed an ex-boyfriend who had come to visit. The Toad had not been on duty but was being called for general information about prison policies.

When the Toad returned three days later he was surprised that he had not received a call from the detective. He went home that day after his shift and found the bed disheveled and the pillow back on the floor. The next day he called Sampson.

"Well, Sampson, what did you find out?"

"What do you mean Leo?"

"What do I mean? I hired you to find out who's been in my house. I came home last night and found evidence that someone had been there. Who was it?"

"Leo," answered Sampson. "I left your house yesterday morning. If someone broke in, it happened after I left."

"Why in hell did you leave? I thought we had an arrangement that you would watch the house for a week?"

"I left because you told me to leave Leo."

"What?" yelled the Toad. The door to the Toad's office was shut but he could be heard all the way to the last office down the hall.

"I never told you to leave."

"Sure you did, Leo. Don't you remember? I was sitting in my car and you walked right up, said hello, told me not to bother about the whole thing and wrote me a check for the entire week. You even apologized for the trouble. As a matter of fact I have the check right here. Still haven't had time to cash it."

"Sampson, are you playing with me?" asked the Toad. "I was out of town."

"Yea, I thought that's what you said earlier," replied Sampson. "I even asked you about it and you said it went a day short."

The Toad sat down in his chair, his jaw working quickly back and forth.

"Leo, you still there?"

"Sampson, I don't get it. I was not home. Are you sure you're not playing some game with me? You cannot afford to do that."

"Leo, we've burned too many bridges together to try and burn our own. Listen, it's not about the money. I haven't cashed the check yet. What's going on?"

"I don't know," sighed the Toad. "Are you really sure it was me? Have you looked at the check's signature?"

"No," answered Sampson. "There's no reason I would have, but I will now. You don't have a twin I don't know about, do you Leo? Cause this guy was pretty much just like you."

The Toad had been slouched in his chair. He sat up quickly.

"What do you mean, pretty much like me?"

"I don't know exactly how to put this Leo except to just say it. He looked like you, he sounded like you, and he dressed like you. But there was one difference."

"What?" asked the Toad, now sitting on the edge of his seat.

"He was nice," answered Sampson. There was a pause in the conversation while one considered the statement and the other considered the result of the statement.

"Could you be a little more precise Sampson?"

"Look, Leo, we've worked together off and on for a number of years. You know me and I know you. It ain't no secret that you're not the friendliest man in town. Not that I care one wit. I'm not either. But you had a big smile on your face. When you walked to the car you were whistling some tune. At the end, just before you left, you patted my arm and said we should get together sometime and go bowling or something."

The Toad pulled the phone back and stared at it as if was infected.

"Bowling? Sampson, I have never bowled a day in my life. Why would I want to bowl with you? Didn't you think that was a bit odd?"

"Of course I did, Leo. But like I said, he looked exactly like you. Look, I'll double check the signatures and let you know if they match. I'll even do a little digging and see if you don't have a secret twin you don't know about. Don't worry about the money. I'll only charge you for the one day at regular rates. I'll send the rest back assuming the signatures match."

"No, I want you to finish the week out and go one more week. I'll send you a check for next week. If this imposter shows I want you to do two things. I want you to approach him and ask him what was the name of the canary from that girl we set up. Only two people know that. You and me. Second, get a picture of the man. I want to see what he looks like."

"You want me to still tail him?" asked Sampson.

"Yes," replied the Toad who then abruptly hung up before Sampson could say anything else.

For the next week and a half Sampson would watch the Toad's house. When the Toad came home after his shift he would approach Sampson and Sampson would ask him the name of the canary. The Toad would answer and Sampson would head home telling the Toad he had nothing to report. The Toad wasn't sure what to make of what had happened but he was glad to come home with nothing changed. He was however not getting much sleep for another reason. Every night just as he was about to drift off, he would hear the sound of a toad croaking. It sounded as if it were coming from somewhere in his room but no matter how thorough the Toad searched he could not find the source. By the second night he had gone over every inch of his house and attic. The third day he hired someone to mow and clean his yard. Then with two days off from work, he found out that during the day he was finally able to get some sleep. The toad still croaked nonstop at night.

One day the Toad was walking down one of the wings of the jail cells. A fresh group of girls had come in, some waiting to be processed and sent back out and some who would finish serving there. The Toad had been so preoccupied with the strange happenings lately that he hadn't had the time to do what he enjoyed best. Looking for his next victim.

Some of the girls were sitting on their bunks. Some were hanging in the back, having heard about the Toad and hoping that by keeping their distance, he would too. At the end of the hallway stood a woman up against the bars, her forearms leaning on a cross bar and her head slightly resting on the bars. The Toad stopped in front of her and stared. He was taken back at first because she seemed to have no fear and the Toad was used to woman shrinking from him whenever he approached. She had stringy dark black hair, pale skin, and dark brown eyes. The Toad made a mental note to find a way to hurt her and turned around to head back.

After a few steps he heard the woman's voice.

"Hey, Toad, it's a shame you had to pay that private eye to watch the house. I could've told you not to bother,"

The Toad froze in his tracks. He composed himself before turning around, subduing both his anger at being called the Toad and alarm that this stranger knew about his personal affairs.

Slowly turning around he walked back to the cell.

"Before you pay a price for what you called me, you're going to tell me how you know about the private detective."

"Why don't you ask Delilah? I hear she'll sing like a canary."

The woman leaned back, holding onto the bars and cackled.

The Toad was speechless.

"What's wrong, Toad? Is there a frog in your throat?"

The woman stepped back a couple of feet, taunting the Toad with her hands like a fighter in a ring baits his opponent. The Toad's face grew bright red as she made kissing sounds with her lips. His eyes bulged wide. He reached for his keys, fumbling in his rage for the right key. He finally found it, then swung open the door, grabbed her by the throat and lifted her up effortlessly against the back wall. She hung by his powerful right arm about a foot off the ground, pinned against the wall. There was a moment of silence as the Toad's flushed face glared at her. Then something happened that the Toad never expected. For a brief moment her face appeared as the face of a large toad. The Toad jumped back instinctively. The woman laughed.

"What's wrong, Toad? Not getting much sleep lately? I know I have. By the way, you need a new pillow." She looked at the Toads belly. "Yours is getting a little out of shape."

The Toad rushed at her only to find he was running blindly into the wall. She was gone. He heard the cell door slam and turned around quickly. The woman was standing outside the door, keys in hand, smiling at the Toad. She swung the ring of keys around her finger.

"Toad, do you know, how many would like to see the look on your face right now? I alone have the privilege. But they're content to know your time is running out."

The woman lifted her head and cried out, "For He shall have judgement without mercy, that hath showed no mercy."

She turned and walked down the hall, whistling and swinging his key ring in one hand.

"You're nothing more than a forgotten snack now, Toad," she called back over her shoulder. "By the way, enjoy the company. Not many here are so fortunate to have so many visitors." She continued whistling until both she and the sound vanished into the air.

The Toad looked down and the floor was covered in toads, croaking and jumping about his feet. The Toad started screaming uncontrollably.

It took about ten minutes for one of the guards to hear him and come running. The Toad was crouched on the small cot, his knees buckled up to his chin.

"Bossman, Bossman, what is it?" shouted the guard as he came running up to the cell. He stopped at the door and looked in, stunned to see his boss crouching in the corner like he had seen so many convicts do over the years. The floor was bare.

"Bossman, what happened? Are you all right? What are you doing in there?"

At first The Toad looked as if he didn't recognize that the guard was even there. He was in shock. Finally, the words of the guard snapped him back to reality and the Toad looked up at the guard, his eyes a bit glazed.

"Open the door," said the Toad weakly. The guard opened the door staring dubiously at the Toad while he exited.

By the time the Toad was out and the door shut, the Toad had composed himself and with an icy look at the guard said, "If you want to live never mention this to anyone."

"Yes, sir, Bossman. Um, just one thing. Do you know where your keys are?"

"No, find them for me and be discreet."

"Yes, Bossman."

The Toad looked at the cell.

"Whose cell is this?"

"No one, Bossman. You want me to move someone here?"

"Yes, fill it. Who was the last occupant here?"

The guard hesitated. "You know, Bossman, that girl who hung herself."

It took a moment and the Toad remembered. There had been a girl whom he had spent almost a year tormenting. She was a very resolute girl, but in time he was able to break her. He thought how perfectly it had worked out that she had hung herself. There was no one to blame. It was just another sad case of a contrite criminal resolving her guilt her own way.

The Toad went back to the office and called Sampson.

"Who did you tell about Delilah?"

"No one, Leo. You're the only one. Why? What happened?"

"Nothing!" growled Leo as he slammed the phone.

That night, Leo stayed in a motel. He needed a night to think and sleep. He was sick of hearing the sound of that toad in his house. The next morning he awoke refreshed and determined that no woman real or imagined was going to get the better of him. He took a shower, put his uniform back on and drove to work. When he reached the outer gate for check-in, he was annoyed that the gate was not open. Normally the guard would see his car coming and would have the gate open before he got there. This was one of the small pleasures the Toad took in his position. He loved the air of importance that it reflected. He also hated small talk. The Toad stopped his car next to the guard house. He rolled his window down and glared at the guard.

"What's wrong with you, Charley? Why isn't the gate opened?"

Charley looked at the man in the car somewhat puzzled that the man knew his name. Then Charley looked at his shirt which had his name stitched on it just above the pocket. Charley smiled.

"Very good, sir," said Charley somewhat bemused. "And how can I help you today, sir? Are you here to see someone?"

"What the devil is wrong with you Charley? Open the gate you fool!" demanded the Toad.

The bemused smile on Charley's face quickly disappeared.

"I don't know who you are mister, but if you call me a fool again, you'll wish you hadn't."

The Toad got nowhere with Charley. Charley had been put off by the man's attitude and he was in no mood to call his superior, so there was nothing for the Toad to do but turn his car around and head back to his house. He expected that by the time he got home his phone would be ringing and they would be asking him why he wasn't in. Charley would be fired, the Toad would see to that. When he got home he found his phone was not ringing. The Toad wanted to wait awhile and let them stew in Charley's own foolishness so he decided to call Sampson. For some reason Sampson was not parked out in front of the Toad's house per their agreement and the irritation in the Toad was piling up.

"DDA, Sampson here. How can I help you?"

"Sampson, why aren't you at my house?" demanded the Toad.

There was a pause on the other end.

"I'm sorry," replied Sampson. "Who is this?"

"It's Leo, you idiot. Who do you think it is? Has everyone gone crazy? Why aren't you at my house?"

But Sampson did not know the Toad either. After some awkward pauses and explosive language on the Toad's part, Sampson slammed his phone down and the Toad was left staring with bewilderment at his phone. He noticed that his hand was shaking. He went to a cabinet and poured himself a drink. He took the drink and the bottle and settled down uneasily into his armchair, placing the bottle on a stand beside him. He took one gulp of his drink and then poured another. This one he casually swirled around with his hand while he stared numbly at the sliding glass door leading to his yard. A great weariness came over him and he fell asleep. Twenty minutes later he awoke quickly because his drink had spilled onto his lap. He looked down at his lap and swore. Then he heard the toad croak. It sounded loud and nearby. He looked up quickly and this time he dropped his glass onto the floor. Staring at him outside the sliding glass door was an enormous eye.

The Toad stood and leaned back, falling backward over his chair. The eye of the creature outside blinked and when it opened its eye a thunderous croak came out so loud that it shattered the glass of the sliding glass door. The Toad scrambled toward the kitchen and ducked behind a counter. He shook his head violently back and forth a few times and slapped his face, trying to wake himself up from what he hoped was a nightmare. For a moment there was silence and the Toad got up the nerve to peer around the corner of the counter. The creature was not there. Slowly the Toad stood and started to walk around the counter. As he did so the face of the creature quickly reappeared and smashed its head directly into the wall of the house. A giant mouth appeared in the living room of the Toad's house. As it opened its mouth it pushed against the ceiling of the house causing the ceiling and roof to shatter and be flung in all directions. Now there was a huge gaping hole and the Toad could see a massive head. The mouth of the creature opened and a long pinkish tongue shot out across the room.

The Toad jumped away from the tongue just in time. The tongue stuck to the refrigerator and yanked it toward the creature's mouth. The Toad watched in horror as the refrigerator went halfway into the creature's mouth. A large forelimb crashed through one of the walls of the house and brushed the refrigerator out of the mouth flinging it to the side. The house was starting to crumble and the Toad turned to flee toward the other end of the house where there was a door that led outside.

As the Toad fled he could hear the house behind him crashing down. He turned his head briefly while he ran and saw a mammoth toad squatting where his house had been. His tongue darted out and just missed reaching him. The Toad ran past the last house on the street and headed toward a field that had tall grass and weeds. He ran wildly, trying to find a place to hide. He saw buildings in the distance and headed toward them.

After a few minutes of running, a large crash was heard about thirty yards to his right. The creature had leaped from the house and landed. The Toad instinctively fell to his face trying his best to hide in the weeds and grass. He was breathing heavily, trying not to make any noise. He heard the grass rustle as the tongue of the creature headed toward him. The Toad jumped up and started running again. Fear propelled him to run beyond his body's abilities. His legs burned with pain but he barely noticed as he raced through the tall weeds. This went on for some time, the Toad managing to evade the tongue of the creature while it hunted him down. He remembered, though he wasn't sure how, that there was a reservoir nearby and that it had a tunnel that ran under a road. He tore into the direction he hoped it would be. He thought if he could hide out in the tunnel long enough perhaps the creature would tire and leave. Eventually he came to the reservoir only to find it blocked with a tall chain fence. It was too tall to climb. He ran along the side of the fence looking for an opening. Just when he was about to give up and go another way he saw a tear in the chain. It was just large enough for him to squeeze through. In the distance he heard the thud of the creature. He started to run down the wall that angled its way to the reservoir bed but tripped and rolled the rest of the way. He landed in a puddle of water and groaned in pain.

The Toad rolled out of the puddle and lay for a moment nursing the scrapes from the cement wall. Then he thought he heard a noise and jumped up and ran as fast as he could toward the tunnel. It was only about twenty yards away but it felt like miles. The thought of safety and rest made him even more conscious of the burning pain that flooded his body. Somehow he managed to reach it and collapsed inside the tunnel. He lay there, unable to move, his chest pounding and his legs feeling as if they would never work again. He sucked in large gulps of air. He could hear the creature landing near him, jumping to and fro, searching for him.

The Toad leaned up against the side of the tunnel and waited, hoping that the creature would move on. Once he had gotten his breath back, he sat and listened intently. It seemed as if the creature might have left. The Toad rested his head against the wall of the tunnel. The irony of the creatures nature was not lost on the Toad. Just the thought of a giant toad smashing his house and leaping hundreds of feet was absurd. Maybe it was a hallucination. And the girl in the cell was also a hallucination. Perhaps none of this was real and he was just losing his mind. He wondered if he had been drugged. Just then he heard music playing. It was on the other side of the tunnel. He couldn't make it out exactly, but it seemed to be some kind of church music. There must be a church on the other side of the tunnel, across the street he thought. The tunnel amplified the noise. He could hear an organ playing. There was some singing, but the words did not make sense and the melody was unfamiliar to him. He had never particularly liked music and he had no use for church music. It was just as well because it would be the last music he would ever hear. It would also be the last sound he would ever hear again, other than screaming, as the tongue of the creature silently slithered its way into the tunnel and latched itself onto the Toad.

CHAPTER 19

The Two Henris

After taking the man to the hospital Henri stayed long enough to ensure that the man's condition had stabilized and that he would recover. He then answered some questions from the local police before making arrangements for the man's car to be taken to a repair shop to be fixed and then brought to the hospital. Henri did not want to stay until the man had recovered because Henri wasn't quite sure how he should deal with the fact that the injured man was his father.

The police were curious that Henri's last name and the last name of the victim were the same but Henri said that it was just a coincidence and that until that day he had never met the man. There was a nervous moment when the police asked for Henri's identification because Henri knew that the date and overall driver's license look would be questioned since it was from a time decades in the future but when he reached into his wallet and pulled it out he noticed that it had changed to the appropriate time period. Later, when he had the opportunity to do so, he noticed that the same thing had happened to his money, which was remarkable since Henri realized he would otherwise have no way of getting around or even buying something to eat.

But Henri did not need the police or anyone else to tell him the identity of the victim. The moment Henri had seen his face he knew that it was the same as the one in the photo he had kept for so many years. It was a peculiar sensation holding the younger head of his father in his hands. At one point, just prior to the doctors taking him away, Henri's father had opened his eyes briefly and looked into Henri's concerned expression. In spite of the ages being reversed it was still the father who gave Henri the comforting smile that everything was going to be okay and not the other way around. Even though Henri had never paid much attention to the driver when he was on the bus, it was clear that the style of the bus was too old to be used in Henri's time. Somehow Henri had stepped back in time to help save his father and somehow the bus driver just happened to be there. If it were not for the bus driver and Henri being there his father would have died. Then it hit Henri. It wasn't fortuitous that the bus driver was there. Henri's presence was something that was orchestrated by a force beyond anything of natural consequence, which at this point he could not understand, but the bus driver's accident had happened years earlier and Henri had at that time not been there to help. What had the bus driver done then without any help? Surely his father would have died. The bus driver had been responsible for his father's death.

Henri had been told by his mother that his father had been killed in a car accident but she had always been vague on details. Years later, when Henri was grown and his uncle had passed away, he hired a private investigator to find out what had happened and discovered that his father had gone missing. It was presumed that for some reason, possibly money problems or another woman, he had simply run off and abandoned his family. He was never seen again. There was no report of any accident and his car had never been found. It had happened the day of Henri's birth. Henri assumed that he was never told because of the embarrassment and hurt it would cause. Henri often thought of how painful it must have been for his mother not only to raise him with no father but to never speak despairingly of him. Henri never told anyone what he had learned. He figured others had to live with the knowledge and it was only fair that he did also.

As Henri drove to a local motel to spend the night he marveled at the strange possibility that he was living in two different times, possibly at once. There was Henri, the boy just born in the hospital. There was this new Henri who had stepped back to the day he was born in order to help his father live. This was not what Henri expected would happen when he drove out to the desert. He really wasn't sure what to expect but certainly not this. He still had not even been to the place where the bus had broken down and he had deserted Elena.

Later that night, he sat reading the front pages of a newspaper as if it were a history book. It occurred to him as he did so that if he were to remain in this time period then he would have about a twelve year wait for the bus to arrive. It was possible Elena was not even born yet. He never knew her exact age. He assumed they were close to the same age. Either way, he had a bit of a wait if he had any hope of seeing the bus again. The thought came to him that he could simply try and go back the way he came and perhaps return to his own time but he felt that he would be deserting Elena's cry for help, whether it had not happened yet, or happened decades ago.

Of course if his father lived that would change everything and it was entirely possible that under this new set of circumstances he would not be on the bus at all, nor would he even be aware of its existence. Presumably he would have grown up with a different set of circumstances and therefore different memories. But no new memories had suddenly come rushing in on him so he had to assume that since he was just as aware of the same things as before then Elena's call for help was just as relevant. The next day he would see if he could locate the place the bus broke down. He remembered that it had been near a gas station and that he had passed one on the way to the hospital. That was a start. He certainly had plenty of time. He would have to do something about money and a place to live and then do what, wait around?

The whole situation seemed ridiculous and impossible. Henri's suitcase was open, resting on the motel bureau. Sitting on top of the clothes in the suitcase was his uncle's Bible. Henri did not remember packing it but he was getting used to things not going normally, so he walked over and picked it up and brought it back to the bed. Henri had never opened it before. He had only kept it as a keepsake from his uncle. He turned the black leather cover to the presentation page. His uncle had written at the top of the page: "My soul waits for the Lord more than the watchmen for the morning; Indeed, more than the watchmen for the morning" (Ps. 130:6). Toward the bottom of the page was written, "Henri, I don't know why this has always been my favorite verse. We wait for many things to happen but our souls are meant to wait for the Lord. I hope this book brings you the answers and hope your soul is waiting for."

Henri felt a little ashamed as he thumbed through the worn pages. He had not read the Bible much and when he did it did not seem to make much sense. What Henri was experiencing did not seem to be something that could be found in the Bible. As a young boy his uncle had sent him to a Bible camp for a week. Some of those Bible stories sounded just as impossible.

Henri turned to the back of the Bible and saw a section labeled "Study Topics." There were sections such as "Verses on Peace" and "Verses on God's Love." Henri's eyes stopped at a section titled "Verses on Guidance." His eyes scanned through some of the verses and rested on one from the Book of Proverbs, "Trust in the Lord with all thine heart and lean not on your own understanding. In all your ways acknowledge Him and He will direct thy paths." "Lean not on your own understanding." That sure seemed to apply here, Henri thought. I wouldn't know where to begin when it came to understanding what is going on. "In all your ways acknowledge Him and He will direct thy paths."

"I suppose I can try that, I guess," Henri said.

Henri tried to say a prayer but he was not quite sure how to word it. He decided instead to read the words out loud. *That's the best I can do*, he thought. Henri put the Bible back on the nightstand and turned off the lights. He closed his eyes and fell into a deep sleep. When he awoke the next morning he had a better idea of what he wanted to do.

In the light of day, it was much easier to locate the gas station. It was a beat up building run by an old man named Gus. An idea had started to form in Henri's mind as he spoke with Gus. The bus had broken down just in front of the gas station. Unless something even stranger happened regarding time, Henri had about a twelve-year wait before the bus would return. Even then he wasn't sure what to expect. But the station would be the best place to wait. Henri spoke with Gus about the possibility of buying the station from Gus. Gus tried to downplay the idea but Henri could see from his initial reaction that Gus was excited about the opportunity. Henri noticed that Gus had a chronic cough and suspected that Gus's health was questionable. That might be one reason that Gus would want some quick money. There was one problem. Henri had brought some money with him but if he were to buy the station and live here for who knew how long, he would need more money.

The idea occurred to Henri that he could go back to practicing medicine but it might be problematic with his medical license. For the moment he let Gus know that he was interested and would be in touch. They shook hands and Henri got into his car. That was another problem that Henri would have to deal with. It was clear from the way Gus was eyeballing Henri's car that Gus had never seen a make like it. For some reason, even though his identification and money had changed to match the times, his car had not. Henri would have to hide the car once he had figured out a way to purchase the gas station.

Henri went back to the motel. There was a diner nearby so Henri decided to get something to eat. As he sat at the counter having a sandwich a radio was playing. Henri was having a good time enjoying some of the songs he knew as "classics" when the station suddenly was changed by the cook. One of the waitresses started to say something but the cook cut her off.

"Four o'clock, Dorothy. Time to hear the races. I got money on Downey's Girl."

Immediately Henri's mind went back to when he was a young boy living with his uncle listening to races. Henri had spent so much time memorizing races that it came back to him as easily as remembering the alphabet. Downey's Girl was a horse that seemed prime to become great. It had a 6–0 record and appeared unbeatable. Then it lost a race to a horse name Ring of Roses, which had never run a race and beat Downey's Girl that day in a huge upset. He remembered that shortly after the race Downey's Girl had mysteriously gone lame and never raced again.

"What's Downey's Girl's record?" asked Henri of the cook.

"She's six wins and no losses and today she's gonna be seven and zip. Why? You got money on another horse?"

"No," answered Henri. "But if I did, I'd put it on Ring of Roses."

"Break Maiden on her first race? You've got to be joking," laughed the cook.

Henri laughed along. "Well, since I don't have any money on it, I have nothing to lose, do I?"

"Tell you what," said the cook. "Your horse wins, I'll buy you lunch."

"And if Downey's Girl wins?" asked Henri.

"When Downey's Girl wins," answered the cook with a wink. "A laugh will be good enough for me."

Henri ate his sandwich, looking down while the race was going on. He had found his answer to how he could buy the gas station. As the horses were about to come down the homestretch Henri stood and looked at the cook.

"Where's the nearest track?" he asked.

The cook answered without turning his head, intently staring at the radio. He waved his hand toward the road.

"About an hour east. Stay on the highway. You'll see signs."

Henri left a tip for the waitress and walked out the door just as the announcer was proclaiming Ring of Roses the winner.

Henri spent the next few weeks jumping from track to track, careful not to wager too much to attract attention. He even lost small amounts on purpose just so that he would not get unduly noticed. By the end of the fourth week, Henri decided to make one large wager and leave. He was amazed at how clearly all of those horse races he had memorized as a child came back to him. When he was young he had wonderful memories sitting with his father placing silly bets on the horses. His father would bet something like a biscuit from the kitchen and Henri would bet a radish from the garden. They would laugh about their winnings and losses.

One day, Henri suggested that he bet the money he had earned that week helping out the veterinarian. He was surprised at the sudden change in his uncle's behavior when he did so. His uncle launched into a tirade on the evils of betting money and how it had ruined peoples families and livelihoods. Henri did not understand it at the time and put it down to his uncle's religion but as he stood at the racetracks trying to get enough money to buy the gas station and put some away he watched different people gambling and he saw firsthand what his uncle had warned him about all those years ago. The looks of desperation on the faces as their horse lost, and their scrambling and begging for the smallest amount of money to try and put back down on a horse. He saw men sitting silently alone wringing their hands and he knew they were wondering what they were going to say to their wife or how they were going to explain to their children why there was no food for supper. By the end of the fourth week he was sick of it all and vowed to never visit a track again. He was not naïve. He had known as an adult that gambling could be a serious addiction that often ruined lives but now he realized that the fond memories of his childhood had clouded the reality. He felt he had no other way to get the money he would need to wait for the bus, but he also had no sympathy for the racetrack owners who encouraged the betting. As far as he was concerned they were as guilty as those just throwing their money away, if not more so.

Henri went back to the gas station and gave Gus the agreed upon money. Henri had heard the type of cough Gus had and knew that Gus did not have long to live. He probably was going to abandon the station anyway. Henri was glad he was able to give him something. Henri had enough money to store away in a safe so that he could live conservatively for the next decade. He hid the car in the garage and bought an inconspicuous old pickup truck he could use for errands. He then went about converting the station into a modest livable home. All that was left was waiting.

CHAPTER 20

At War with the Beast

Catherine did not know the exact count but it seemed as if it had been a long time since anyone had exited the bus. One thing she knew for certain was the three who had not left: Elena, the stranger, and the creature. She had made attempts to look through the windows but the inside seemed to be filled with a thick, dark mist. She tried to pound on the window where the stranger sat, hoping he would answer or at least acknowledge her, but it was to no avail. Catherine felt useless but not without hope. She lay down on the rock and rested her head on her arm. She drifted into a light sleep, when suddenly she thought that she felt something touch her.

She sat up quickly only to find the entire area covered in a thick blackness. At first Catherine thought the bus might have caught on fire but it wasn't smoke that enveloped her. She was able to breathe. However, it was incredibly oppressive and overwhelming. She could not see her hand in front of her face and she had no sense of the location of the bus. Her only physical reference point was the rock. Keeping her hands on the rock, Catherine fell to her knees and leaned on the rock in prayer.

It felt as if the smoke was a presence. There was an ugliness to it that seemed to glory in its depravity. At times it felt as if parts of the blackness formed itself into hands and would either buffet her or try to grab her. She called out to the Lord, her words barely leaving her lips before they were swallowed up in the evil around her. She closed her eyes as tight as she could and tried to picture Elena while she prayed.

As she prayed, she could feel the blackness sometimes brush against her like an angry person pushing their way through a crowd. Sometimes it almost seemed to be trying to grasp her by the feet or arms and pull on her. The mother was petrified but determined to focus on Elena. She also tried to focus on the face of her Savior when He had looked down on her earlier. When she was able to do so, the blackness seemed to briefly back away.

Then the noises came. First it was gently laughing. Not a familiar friendly laughter, but a wicked, mocking sinister laugh. Then every horrible accusation imaginable assaulted her mind. Perverse, self-serving, and destructive thoughts flooded her with vile images. She tried to keep her attention on His face but she felt like someone holding onto a kite in a gale wind.

Catherine did not know how much longer she could continue. If the blackness continued it would not only be around her but it would find its way into her. Eventually, she thought, it would fill her being and all that she was would disappear and only the blackness would remain.

"Jesus," she whispered. The words could barely be heard by her. She was not even sure that the word had found its way out of her mouth.

"Jesus," she said again. This time she could hear her own voice. It was as if a small place was cleared away around her face and she had some room to breathe. She felt a thud on her back from the blackness as it repeatedly struck her.

"Jesus, Jesus, Elena, Jesus, Elena!" she cried out.

Suddenly a bright light broke through the bus windows and lit up the area around her.

In the bus it was evening and with the exception of the Gatekeeper, Elena, and the creature, who in ancient times was known as the beast, all had either voluntarily abandoned the bus or had in one way or another been dismissed. Some who were gone had simply disappeared in the night. A few had attempted to engage the pale visitor in conversation, trying to ascertain who or even what he was and what was his purpose on the bus. The beast was there for a specific purpose. However that purpose did not involve answering questions from those he deemed insignificant, and those few who had dared pursue a conversation simply vanished while others slept at night. It did not take long for the remaining passengers to get the point and the visitor was left alone. It even drove some to flee the bus. While this was not the beast's purpose he knew that in the end only those who remained would matter. Shortly after Henri had left, Elena had fallen mercifully into a deep sleep and continued to remain curled up on the seat while much of the drama with the other passengers played its part. The Gatekeeper maintained his peace.

On the evening of the fourth night, Elena slowly opened her eyes, yawned silently, and rubbed the sleep away from her eyes. She looked to the front of the bus to see the stranger smiling at her, his eyes seeming to light up his face. There was, however, a fierceness to the stranger that she didn't notice before. His presence caused her want to draw near and pull back at the same time. All of the other seats around her were empty. Elena turned around and saw the beast. He too had a smile. This one was barely visible but it was clear it was not an inviting smile of friendship but the type of smile one might imagine a predator would have when it senses it will soon have its prey in his teeth. Even in the darkness of the bus the beast's skin seemed to have an almost pale glow and she could see that the wrinkles on the face appeared unnatural. It was faint, but she could see evenly spaced horizontal wrinkles or ridges starting at the top of his head and running down his face and neck. The pupil and the iris had merged into a small black circle that enlarged just a fraction when the beast had smiled. The beast sat perfectly still but Elena had the distinct impression that the beast intended to soon come after her in some manner. She slowly slid to the floor onto her knees and then crawled under the seat in front of her.

Elena heard a noise coming from the front of the bus. She poked her head into the aisle and saw the Gatekeeper standing, facing them with a sense of purity and purpose. He stepped into the aisle and walked toward the back of the bus. Elena cowered in fear but peeked out just enough to see the Gatekeeper's face as he passed. He gave her a slight wink and Elena felt such a sense of peace and joy that she almost giggled.

The Gatekeeper continued at an even pace toward the beast. When he reached him, the beast moved for the first time since he boarded the bus. In contrast to the Gatekeeper, the beast rose slowly and awkwardly. It was an odd and unnatural movement. The beast stood to face the Gatekeeper, who had turned slightly so that his back was angled, directly blocking Elena.

"You can go," dismissed the beast in a guttural voice. "You are no longer wanted or needed."

"Only One tells me to go or to stay," replied the Gatekeeper almost cheerfully.

The beast snarled "You are not as powerful as you presume Gatekeeper. I moved past you with little effort."

The Gatekeeper's expression did not change. "You no more crept pass me here than you did in the garden. You are here, like everyone else, by permission and purpose."

"She is mine," roared the beast with black, rotten spit flinging from his lips. "Her father was mine and she is mine."

Elena curled up as tight as she could under the seat. Her body was shaking and her mind was racing trying to understand just what the words meant. She held her breath and felt frozen in eternity, fearful of what would happen. The Gatekeeper waited patiently while eternity held its breath.

"Her father was yours by choice, Beast." The Gatekeeper turned around and smiled at Elena. "I don't believe she has made the same decision," he said as he turned back at the beast.

"You are no one to stop me," growled the beast. "You are a puppet."

The Gatekeeper's frame seemed to enlarge and whiten.

The Gatekeeper lifted up his hands and cried out, "Lift up your heads, you gates; be lifted up, you ancient doors, that the King of glory may come in. Who is this King of glory? The Lord strong and mighty, the Lord mighty in battle. Lift up your heads, you gates; lift them up, you ancient doors, that the King of glory may come in."

For a moment, the bus lit up with a light brighter than anything Elena had ever seen or imagined. The bus was filled with a sense of majesty and triumph and the beast leaned back briefly, but quickly recovered. He hissed slowly and deliberately at the Gatekeeper. There was a sense of victory looming as it spoke its next words.

"Quote that book all you want. It doesn't change anything. Her mother has abandoned her. You cannot claim her by right. I am claiming her by default and by force if necessary."

Just as the beast was about to leap onto the Gatekeeper a voice was heard from the front of the bus. It was Elena's mother.

"You cannot claim what you do not have a right to," cried the mother from the other end of the bus. Elena looked up and saw her mother standing at the front of the bus. She had a look on her face that Elena had only seen on the faces of warriors and gallant knights in storybooks she had read. There was a holy fierceness to her.

The mother returned Elena's look possibly for the first time in her life. There was never a painting so beautiful or a sunset as majestic as Elena's face at that moment. She had always tried to avoid looking at Elena, but now, except for the duty which was at hand, she would have been content to never turn away.

Catherine faced the beast like a soldier about to charge the enemy. The loving look Elena's mother had just given her changed to ferocious fury as she raced fearlessly down the aisle, arms outstretched and her hands extended as if they were swords. The Gatekeeper turned to the side as she tore past him and flung herself onto the beast. The beast fell backward from the surprising force of the mother. She straddled his chest and with blind rage tore away at his face. She felt absolute abandonment to perfect hatred. This was not the same hate she had experienced at those who had hurt her in the past. That hatred was weak and motivated by self-pity. This was a holy indignation and she was engulfed in it. As she tore away at the beast's face, the beast slowly started to shrink until he was gone. The worm, so small it was invisible to all but the Gatekeeper, slithered along the side of the bus and down the steps.

Catherine, sitting alone on the floor and breathing heavily, turned with a confused look to the Gatekeeper.

"What happened to it?" she asked.

"It is gone," answered the Gatekeeper. "He was not expecting you. Presumption has always been his greatest weakness. In spite of all he has seen regarding redemption, he is always surprised by its power. He has no authority over the wrath of the Lamb. He will seek others to devour. He is blinded by an insatiable hunger and that is what he is driven to do."

Catherine jumped up and ran to Elena and held her, both with tears streaming down their faces. The mother kept kissing her daughter's cheeks and neck. She sobbed apologies until they were both exhausted from joy. They both sat back with Elena resting in her mother's arms. The Gatekeeper walked toward them and faced Elena.

"I will leave now with your permission," he said as nodded solemnly at Elena.

Elena smiled and nodded back.

As the Gatekeeper reached the front of the bus he turned around and looked playfully back at Elena.

"By the way, you have someone waiting for you outside. By your standards he has been there a very long time."

Outside, the sun was just starting to set. Henri was at his desk, head down, and reading his uncle's Bible with pen in hand, as he had for years in front of the garage window when the green light came on and he reached for the camera. It was the bus.

His pen rolled unconsciously off his fingers and Henri stood slowly, almost afraid that movement might cause it to disappear. He stared, hypnotized by the nonchalance of its presence. He was never quite sure what to expect or what he should do when whatever it was that he might expect should actually happen. After some time he reasoned that he did not cause the bus to appear and therefore it was unlikely that it would disappear or take off so he decided to open the front door and walk out. He approached the bus and as he did so, his eyes were scanning from front to back to see if he could see either the bus driver or any of the passengers. At first it appeared that no one was on the bus and the idea occurred to him that maybe he was supposed to board the bus, something he was not sure he wanted to do. But then he spotted the heads of two passengers on the opposite side of the isle who both, by their size, appeared to be adults. He stood still.

Even though he could not identify either of the two passengers he could see that their bodies were facing toward the front of the bus and it seemed to him that they were looking at someone, possibly even talking to someone at the front—a person whom Henri could not see. Then one of the passengers turned toward Henri. The glare on the glass from the setting sun made it impossible for Henri to clearly see anyone's face but he could see the passenger facing him take hurried steps toward the front door. Henri stared breathlessly, his heart pounding as the door opened.

An old woman stepped out. She appeared to be about Henri's age. She had her hand gently on the rail as she gingerly walked down the steps of the bus. For a moment Henri almost warned her about stepping on the ground lest she vanish, but he held off. The woman herself seemed to pause, as if thinking the same thought as Henri. She then closed her eyes and took in a deep breath. Opening her eyes she gazed up at the brilliant orange sunset, slowly exhaling as if she were enjoying her first breath of fresh air after a long wait. She scanned the desert around her with what seemed like love and appreciation, and then she gave a strange look at the gas station as if she expected it to appear differently. Once finished with this greeting to all that lay before her, her gaze went back to the ground, contemplating its power. Then suddenly she looked at Henri, smiled, and stepped off the bus.

Henri could not remember an older lady on the bus. He remembered an elderly couple who had stepped off the bus with a joy that was contrary to everyone else's fearful leap. However, he didn't recognize this woman. But once she smiled at Henri, he knew immediately who she was. Age could not hide the once forgotten smile of Elena.

Elena looked straight at Henri as she stepped onto the ground. She thought to herself that if she disappeared she wanted it to happen while she was looking at Henri. She was equally surprised by Henri's appearance, but she knew the moment that the Gatekeeper had told her someone was waiting that it would be Henri. Shortly after she touched the ground Henri came face to face with her. Elena looked down at her wrinkled hands and saw how aged they appeared. She felt her hair and gently skimmed the lines on her face. It felt strange to feel so old. She was not afraid and it comforted her to see Henri also looking old. She knew he would find her. She held up her hand and looked at the back of it.

"So this is what happens when you leave," she said.

Henri opened his eyes a little wider.

"You're speaking!"

Elena laughed. It did not occur to her that she had actually said the words that she was thinking. Normally, she would have taken that thought and either attempted to mime the thought or start drawing on her board, which she then realized was no longer about her neck. It was an unusual experience, to say the least, to hear your own voice for the first time. Her first instinct had been to look around to see who had spoken the words.

"How wonderful and strange," she said slowly, savoring the sound of her voice. "But why are we so old?"

"I don't know," answered Henri. "I remained the same age when I left. So did my uncle. How long were you in the bus? How many years has it been?"

"It has only been a few days since you left," said Elena.

"How can that be? I have been off the bus for decades," answered Henri. "I have lived a whole life. I had forgotten everything until twelve years ago when I saw your message. I have been waiting here since then."

"What message?" asked Elena.

Henri walked Elena into the building and showed her the photograph of her sitting on the bus seat with the chalkboard around her neck.

"I wrote that after you left a couple of days ago," said Elena. "You have been here for twelve years?"

"Yes. I have been waiting, though I wasn't sure for what."

Henri showed Elena around the room and pointed out the photographs he had taken of the ghostly images exiting the bus. Some they both felt they recognized. They went back outside and Elena saw the flat rock nearby that she had seen from the bus. It looked comfortable and she asked Henri if he would mind sitting down for a while. As they did, Henri told her what had happened to him, passing out in the desert and being found by his uncle, and losing all memory of what had taken place on the bus. He told her of his life and how he had come to be back here. Then he told her of the bus driver and his father.

"The bus driver left," stated Elena. "Everyone left." Then her eyes lit up. "My mother is back," she said excitedly.

"How can this be?" said Henri. "I don't understand."

Elena looked at Henri and smiled. "My mother is back and your father is alive."

"And we are old."

"And we are old," laughed Elena. "But I think we are supposed to go back onto the bus. There is something different about my mother. I think we are meant to have a life together. A very good life. I cannot imagine that happening if I am to be old."

Henri sat still for a long time. The one thing that had bothered him through these years of waiting was the possibility of another Henri growing up somewhere with his father. He had no memory of his father. The other Henri would have separate memories not only of his father, but also of his mother and probably his uncle. It somehow seemed wrong that there was a possibility of two of him alive at the same time. It seemed to Henri that the only way to reconcile this odd paradox was to get back on the bus.

"Yes, I want to be back on the bus too," said Henri. He took Elena's hand and they walked toward the bus. Elena stepped into the bus first and as Henri started up the steps he looked back at the building that had been his makeshift home the last ten years. As he was looking he could see the building fading away until it blended into the desert and the sunset. When Henri turned around he saw the young face of Elena smiling back at him, her chalkboard strung around her neck, and her small hand still holding onto the hand of a young boy. The bus door closed and all that remained was the distant sound of traffic on the new highway.

CHAPTER 21

"And Their Sins and Iniquities I Will Remember No More"
(Heb. 10:17)

The bus driver squatted down in front of one of the buses rear tires, running his hand slowly along the thick tread down near the base of the tire, feeling carefully until his hand felt the tip of the head of a nail wedged between the rows of rubber. He dug his fingernail deep into the tread and pulled the long part of the nail, which had been wedged neatly in the groove of the tread. The nail did not put up a fight and slid out without much effort. He took his flashlight and ducked his head under the back of the bus. Then because it was uncomfortable being hunched down on legs, he rolled on his back and lay with his head looking up. He shined his light at the tire to make sure that there was no damage from the nail and when he was satisfied with the effectiveness of his surgical skills, he aimed his light at the undercarriage of the bus. There was a small dent in the exhaust pipe but other than that everything seemed to be in order. He smiled. It felt good to be a bus driver again.

He grunted a little as he shimmied his way out from underneath the back of the bus and he picked up his clipboard next to the tire. Checking off the remaining boxes on his equipment list, he thought of how far he had come. He considered himself lucky. After being suspended without pay for two years due to the accident, he was finally back as a full-time driver returning to the same route he had started twelve years earlier. For two years he had picked up odd jobs, doing whatever he could to make ends meet while helping out at home with his mother; everything from being a dishwasher to doing janitorial work. When he was finally reinstated, it was only on a part time basis while he served a probationary period. Eventually he was able to drive full time. It some ways it was just like starting over. Initially he was forced to take whatever routes were available but in time he was able to return to his original route.

Over time, in spite of his best efforts to try and recall details, the bus driver had slowly forgotten the events that had happened on the bus. Like a dream that becomes less and less clear, the bus driver simply forgot all but the last truth. He had almost killed a man. While the memories had still been fresh he never told anyone, not even the man he had hit with his bus. How could he? Who would believe him? To him, the events that occurred during those four days on the bus were a fantastical series of events along with characters that had presented him with a mystery that he would never in this life be able to unravel. Yet he also knew that if he spoke to others about what had happened it would only make him sound as if he had lost his mind, an idea he had often felt might be true. So he kept the secret of his mystery to himself and away from others. As the details of the mystery gradually dissipated in his memory it eventually became a secret also to him. Now, when he thought of the awful events of that evening he was grateful that through the help of the doctor who had suddenly drifted in and then out of his life, he had been able to get the man to the hospital in time to save him.

One thing that never left him was the feeling he had while pulling the man out of the bushes. He could never forget the intense but brief suggestion that came to him of not helping the man but somehow hiding what had happened. In the end that momentary foolish consideration of self-preservation would have most certainly haunted him the rest of his days. It was a shuddering thought that never left him. Somehow, by God's grace, he had done the right thing. Accidents happen, he reminded himself, but decisions are made.

But often out of every tragedy comes an unexpected blessing and for the bus driver it was Adiya. When he saw her in the hospital he did not ask how she had gotten there. He knew that she probably did not know herself. Only the Gatekeeper could answer that question. But he knew he was the one the Gatekeeper chose to use to rescue her. So he adopted her as his own daughter. He told his mother that she had been abandoned on the side of the road and he had brought her to the hospital. At first Adiya spoke very little. Nothing more than "yes," "no," and "thank you." But she confirmed the bus driver's story to everyone and since no one could either dispute it or find her real parents she was eventually formally adopted into the family. As time went on and the bus driver forgot the strange events on the bus the story he told his mother was the story he came to also believe.

After checking out the bus, the driver waited by the door as people began boarding. He tore their tickets and gave out "hellos" and smiles. There was a small girl with a chalkboard strung around her neck with a woman. They smiled warmly and gave him their tickets. The girl paused and wrote something on the chalkboard and showed it to the bus driver.

"Drive carefully," she wrote.

The bus driver laughed and tipped his hat.

"Yes, ma'am," he said.

A few others got on the bus. The last two were a young boy and a man. The bus driver recognized the man immediately.

"Why, Joe, it's you. It's so good to see you. How long has it been?"

The boy in front of Joe went up the stairs quickly and found a seat near the window across the aisle from the girl and her mother. He looked out the window with boyhood interest. Since there were no more passengers to board, the bus driver and Joe talked. The bus driver had done everything he could after the accident to help Joe during his recovery but eventually Joe had gotten better and left the hospital to be with his wife and newborn.

"It's been years, hasn't it," said Joe. "I'm doing well. I see you got your route back. I'm glad for you."

There was a short pause as both men stood.

"So what brings you out this way?" asked the bus driver.

Joe looked through one of the windows and watched his son find a seat.

"Molly died recently from a brain tumor and I've decided to visit my brother. I thought getting away might help my son Henri. It's been a difficult time."

"I'm so sorry to hear that Joe. If there is anything I can do to help, please don't hesitate…" His voice trailed off and there was an awkward silence. Joe put his hand on the bus driver's shoulder.

"Thanks. It's good to see you again."

Joe handed the ticket stub to the bus driver and boarded the bus. The bus driver looked around one last time and climbed the steps to his seat. He adjusted his mirror and looked back at the people on the bus. He smiled sadly at Joe and his son and then started the engine.

Elena sat next to her mother. Her mother had her arm around Elena and was watching her write on her chalkboard. When Elena was done she turned around and faced Henri. Henri looked at her and smiled. Then he looked at the chalkboard.

"Hello, I'm Elena," it said. There was a picture of a boy on it that Henri guessed must be him and he laughed.

"Hi. I'm Henri," he answered.

Elena's mother turned around and smiled at the boy and his father.

"Hello, my name is Kay. This is my daughter, whose name you now know."

The man smiled and looked at Kay.

"Hello. My name is Auberon, but most people call me Joe. And you now know my son Henri."

Kay laughed a little. Auberon looked at her with a puzzled expression.

"I'm sorry," said Kay. "It's just that you told me your full name and then your nickname. Kay is my nickname, but my full name is Catherine. I like Auberon, though."

"I like Catherine," responded Auberon. "Where are you heading, Catherine?"

Catherine looked at Elena and gently brushed a strand of her hair away from her face. She gazed into her beautifully round redemptive eyes with delicately long lashes and wanted to weep with joy. After a moment, she looked at Auberon and smiled.

"I don't know. We're kind of starting over. We were thinking of heading east."

Elena affectionately grabbed her mother's hand and leaned on her shoulder.

"Well," answered Auberon. "We're out to visit my brother. Henri has never met his uncle. They have a wonderful farm near a lake. While you're thinking where you would like to start over, you're welcome to visit anytime as our guest."

"That's very kind of you," said Catherine. "Very kind."

The passengers felt a slight lurch as the bus driver pulled away from the station and turned toward the highway.

CPSIA information can be obtained
at www.ICGtesting.com
Printed in the USA
BVHW081114020521
606285BV00006B/251

9 781098 077921